SPELLS AND SUSPICIONS

CHARMED AND DANGEROUS BOOK 3

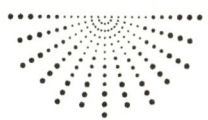

MORGAN VALE

SPELLS AND SUSPICIONS

A pumpkin pie to die for...

When the biggest baking competition around comes to Haven, Kat's cousin Emily is ready to taste sweet victory. But the event turns sour when a judge keels over — seemingly poisoned by her pumpkin pie!

With Emily's innocence at stake, Kat takes action. Delving deep into the world of competitive baking, she'll have to use more than a few tricks and treats to get to the bottom of things. Each contestant has something to hide, and any of them could have done it — which baker isn't as sweet as they seem?

Join Kat, her black cat Albus, and her quirky friends as they embark on this deliciously dangerous adventure. Because this time, the desserts really are to die for.

Spells and Suspicions is the third book in the Charmed and Dangerous paranormal cozy mystery series. These are clean reads with no swearing, gore, or adult situations, so curl up and enjoy!

Spells and Suspicions

My name is Kat, and I'm a witch. An earth witch, to be exact. The Curious Cauldron, my store, houses all kinds of herbs, teas, and tinctures brewed by yours truly and infused with my own special brand of magic.

So when my cousin Emily came calling asking for baking help, she should have known she was barking up the wrong tree.

"Wait, wait, wait...explain this to me again?"

Emily pouted and stuck out her lip. I'd been listening, but she talked so fast my ears hadn't had time to catch up.

"Remember that cooking competition I applied for — the Harvest Baking Championship?"

"Yeah?"

"I got in!"

"What?! No way!" I put down the sachet in my hands and drew her into a hug. "That's such great news!"

"I could hardly believe it myself," she agreed, squeezing me tight. "This is going to put my business on the map, Kat. This is going to put *Haven* on the map."

"Why Haven?"

"Because." Her flushed face made her look like she was about to burst from excitement. "Haven won the draw to host the show!"

I blinked. "Right here? As in, this Haven? We barely show up on any maps!"

"Yes, this Haven. What other place would I be talking about?"

"I just thought they'd pick a bigger city."

Emily shrugged. "They wanted it to be at one of the baker's hometowns. Give it that down to earth feel. All the towns were put in a hat and Haven won the luck of the draw."

"How about that," I said, though my mind was already racing with possibilities.

"You know what this means," Emily beamed.

"Tourists?"

She nodded. "And a lot of them." Emily clapped her hands together. "Don't you see, if we play our cards right..." Her eyes shone and she was practically bouncing up and down on the balls of her feet. "We'll be sitting pretty by the end of this just by all the extra publicity. If we win...even better."

I stopped her right there. "Wait a second. What's this 'we'?"

Emily gazed down at her feet and stopped bouncing. Her throat bobbed with a deep breath. "That's, um, the other thing I wanted to ask you about. Usually, you know I work with Pablo on big projects like this one. But he had to have literally the worst timing on Earth and can't make it during the scheduled dates." She wrung her hands, the former excitement all but gone. "I have been asking around trying to find someone else, but it's such short notice and it's the busiest time of year for most folks here in Haven..."

Now I saw where she was trying to go with this. "You think I'm the one to help?" I said incredulously. "You *do* remember the custard incident, right?"

Emily snorted at the memory of our childhood. "That was years ago." She brushed it off as nothing more than a bygone joke. "And we got it off the ceiling eventually, didn't we?"

I groaned and smacked a hand to my forehead. Sometimes there was just no getting through to her. But then again, she and I had that in common: stubborn as a rock.

"That's not the point," I started, even though I knew I'd already lost. "I know how important this is to you, and I don't want to let you down. My baking skills are...average at best. Custard incident at worst." I winked.

"Look at me, Kat." Emily snapped her fingers to get my attention. "Would I even be here if I thought you were gonna let me down? You're better than you give yourself credit for, and you've helped me in the kitchen before." She crossed her arms. "I don't want some stranger there that I don't mesh with. I want you."

I admired her confidence in me, even though I didn't share the same faith. But she was right in one place, at least: we'd always been there for each other through thick and thin. Why not now?

"I'll think about it," I said finally. I shifted back and forth on my feet, my hands fidgeting at my sides. Did she really know what she was getting herself into?

Emily simply gave me a calm, friendly smile. "All right. I appreciate it, Kat. I do hope you say yes." Her grin grew larger. "I mean, no pressure, but if I can't find a partner, I can't compete, so..."

I rolled my eyes. "You call that no pressure?"

"I'm just saying!" Emily protested.

Seeing there was no way I was gonna get around this, I relented. "When do you need to know by?"

"Friday."

I gulped. Theoretically, I guess I *could*, though I'd have to adjust my schedule at the shop and ideally brush up on my cooking skills. "All right. I'll let you know."

"Promise?" She crooned in her sweetest voice.

"Pinky promise," I agreed. We locked our little fingers together like we were kids again, and that was that.

"See ya this weekend!" She turned and waved before heading to the door. "I think I left the oven running!"

The door chimed to announce her exit, leaving me standing there behind the counter, more than a little dumbstruck and more than a little full of ideas.

"You okay?" Albus woke up from his nap and padded over to the counter, noticing my far-off expression. "I heard something about food."

I barked out a laugh. "Of course you did."

"Well, what was it?" He hopped up and nudged me. Pay no mind to the fact that I had some very fragile dried herbs in my hands.

Familiars didn't care.

"It was just Emily. She said there's a baking competition coming to Haven, and she's looking for a partner."

Albus stopped sniffing my hands and perked up, ears pointing toward the sky. "Wait, are you talking about *the* Harvest Baking Championship?"

Seriously, did everyone know about this thing but me?

"Um, yeah?"

"And she wants *you* to be her partner." Albus sneezed — his version of a laugh. "That's rich."

"Hey!" I protested and put my hands on my hips. "I'm not *that* bad. And Emily trusts me, so that's gotta count for something right?"

"Kat, Kat, Kat..." Albus shook his head back and forth. "Might I remind you of the custard incident?"

I threw my hands up in the air. "Why won't anyone let that go?!"

CHAPTER TWO

THE DAY OF THE COMPETITION

"Am I making a horrible mistake?" I looked myself in the mirror and pulled my hair back into a ponytail.

My grandma Crystal stood next to me, a hand on my shoulder. "There's one way to find out." Her eyes twinkled.

"Yeah," I conceded. "I just hope Emily won't hate me if I mess this up."

"Oh hush with that," she swatted at my shoulder playfully. "You know your thoughts are things, right? The more you put them out there, the more they find their way into reality."

I sighed. I knew she was right, but I couldn't help worrying — this was the biggest opportunity of Emily's career, and possibly mine as well.

"Now you look lovely. Go out there and go get 'em. I'll be watching."

"Thank you, grandma." I gave her a hug.

"What's life without a little risk?" She quips. "Boring, that's what. Now go show 'em what Haven's made of."

She clapped me on the back and off I went.

It didn't take long for me to find Emily. In fact, I didn't have to find her at all — the moment I opened my front door, she stood there, stricken with panic.

"Emily!" I gasped and ushered her inside. "What is going on? I was just about to go pick you up."

"My...cookbook..." She gasped and doubled over, hands on her knees. Had she *run* all the way over here?

"Which cookbook? Are you sure it's not on the shelf at Crafty Cakes?"

If 'bless your heart' had a facial expression, Emily had just nailed it. "Kat," she said slowly as if I was deaf. "My *cookbook*. You know, the one all kitchen witches have? My *spell* book?"

Oh, duh. Each kitchen witch kept a grimoire of recipes, ingredients, and experiments. They drew their power from those fabled tomes and immortalized each creation within the pages. Yes, losing *that* cookbook would be a problem indeed.

"Where did you last see it?" I didn't know what else to say. Everything else sounded super lame.

"Ugh, the same place it always is. Next to the other cookbooks in the back."

"Could someone have borrowed it?"

"Like who?" She raised an eyebrow. "It's magically sealed, so they wouldn't find it much good anyway."

"I don't know, Emily." I wrung my hands. "I'm just trying to help."

"I know. I know." She hugged her arms around herself and let out a deep breath. "I'm just all amped up about the competition, and now that it's finally the day I can't find the darn thing. If we don't hurry we're going to be late!"

"All right." I put a steadying hand on her shoulder. "First, deep breaths. I know you're attached to your spellbook but it's better to be there without it than not be there at all, right?"

Emily slumped. "Right."

"And you're a great witch, Em. More than you give yourself credit for. I bet you don't even need that old thing to blast the other bakers out of the water."

Her lips turned up into a grin at that. "I hope you're right. Now let's get over there."

As we rushed out the door and to the car, Albus had to slip in one last comment.

"Sugar, spice, and everything nice...that's what witches are made of."

The Harvest Baking Championship took place in a large open valley surrounded by forests and mountains on either side. The looming Appalachians watched over us and a slight chill in the air still hung around, even though the fog had all but burnt away.

The organizers had set up four baking stations on the lawn, each outfitted with the latest ovens, mixers, and other equipment. A few spices and staples rested in a small pantry on each station. The rest of the ingredients lived in a large communal fridge near the judge's table.

I gulped as I realized the gravity of the situation. This was just like the cooking shows my mom liked to watch on TV. Only this time, it was real. Emily and I would not be spectators. This time, we were actually participating.

In just a few short moments, one of those glittering cooking stations would be hers.

No, scratch that — *ours*.

"Over here," Emily grabbed my arm and pointed to a table where a small line formed. I yanked my eyes away from the scene and followed her, Albus keeping pace underfoot.

We approached the registration table and got in line behind two other bakers.

When a man in an eye-blindingly bright orange suit crossed in front of us, Emily gasped.

"Do you know who that is?" She hissed as soon as he passed.

"Uh...no?" I was already feeling out-of-place enough at this competition. I didn't live and breathe baking like the others here. And apparently, I didn't recognize any of the big names, either.

"That's Fabio Androna!" Emily nearly squealed. "I've been following his work ever since he was featured in *Kitchen Witch Weekly* — I never thought I'd actually get to meet him."

"Whoa." I didn't have to try to exaggerate — that *did* sound impressive. But there was that nagging feeling again that I didn't belong. Who was I next to someone like Fabio?

Just then, the woman in front of us in the queue turned. She crossed her arms and looked down her nose at us, lip curling up in a slight sneer. "Will you two fangirls keep it down? I'm trying to focus."

I froze. Focus on what?

"If you think you have a shot at impressing Fabio,

think again. I'm the only one that's going to do that today."

Emily tensed next to me and my instincts kicked in. "And what makes you think that?" I said, though it came off a little more combative than I intended.

The woman scoffed. She pointed at the embroidery on her crisp white shirt. "Can you even read? I'm Meryl Mason, the best baker this side of the Mississippi. And you are...?"

"Emily Morris," Em nudged me aside and cut in, her expression just as fierce. "And this here's my cousin Kat Sullivan."

"Hmm," she tapped her chin. "Can't say I've heard of you. I've been on the competition circuit for years and I know all the regulars. You? You're not one of them."

"Maybe because I've been spending my time baking instead of bragging about it."

I sucked in a breath. Ooh, Emily had sass today!

"I guess we'll see who comes out on top," Meryl replied. Her face was all smiles, but the venom beneath spoiled it. "Oh, would you look at that? It's my turn. I'll be seeing you."

With a prissy wave, she stepped up to the registration table and left us both with our mouths hanging open.

I shot a glare at Emily. Her shoulders were still

tensed up around her ears, her hands balled into fists. "Em," I said gently, "chill."

"Of course *she* had to be here." With some effort, she unclenched her shoulders and fists, giving me an apologetic look. "Sorry. That's Meryl. She's...well, a real *witch*, if you know what I mean."

"You know her?"

"Only from the press. She's one of those 'any press is good press' kind of people. The number of crazy stunts she's pulled for attention..." Emily shook her head. "I just hope she doesn't try anything here today."

"She better not." I shook my head. "I've had enough drama for a lifetime lately."

"Isn't that the truth," Emily agreed. "Okay, looks like it's our turn. Let's go."

We stepped up to the registration table where an older man and woman sat with clipboards.

"Name?" The man asked. The competition only had four teams — it shouldn't have been that hard to figure out. Especially considering there was only one welcome packet left on the table. Ours.

"Emily Morris."

He checked the list. "Ah, so you're the hometown baking queen." Striking through her name with a highlighter, he paused, then squinted at me.

"Excuse me, Miss Morris, but who is this with you?"

"This is my cousin, Kat Sullivan. She's agreed to be my partner."

The man frowned. He leaned across the table to confer with the other woman at the table, but their voices were too low to make out any words. My heart thudded hard for a few beats. Surely she'd told them about me?

"I'm sorry," the man said after turning back to us. His face didn't look sorry at all. Pushing the clipboard toward us, he pointed at a line of fine print. "Didn't you receive the revised rules? This will be a solo competition. No partners allowed."

The realization hit me like a punch in the gut. Emily tensed next to me. "What?"

"You heard me," the man said, unamused. "Either you compete alone, or not at all."

I frowned. Talk about a hard choice. "Give us a moment." I pulled Emily to the side and tried to get a read on her reaction.

"I'm so sorry, Kat." Emily's eyes glistened. "This must have been a last-minute change. I swear I didn't know."

I sighed. "I get it. Rules are rules. No matter how much we hate them." I kicked at a clod of dirt. And boy, did I hate them.

"I can't decide what to do. I don't want to leave you out, but I've been planning for this day for so long..." She shifted back and forth on the balls of her feet. I wished I could make the decision for her, but I knew I couldn't.

"You know what?" I put an arm around her shoulder. "Forget all this. You're the best baker in town, and I know you'll do great."

"You really think so?" Emily said. "Should I go for it?"

I tilted my head toward the stations where the bakers gathered. In particular, I shot a few eye-daggers at Meryl, our snobby competitor. "It's up to you, but I'd want to compete just to wipe the smirk off her face." I jerked a thumb in Meryl's direction, but she was too absorbed in conversation to notice.

That made Emily smile. "You're right. I don't give myself enough credit. Who does she think she is, anyway?"

"The Great and Powerful Meryl Mason, of course." I exaggerated the words and waved my hands in a flamboyant gesture. "Wouldn't want to ruin her flawless reputation."

Emily rolled her eyes. With that, she made up her mind. "I'm gonna do it." Her voice lost all trace of insecurity, now firm and determined. "I came this far and I'm not throwing away my shot."

"That's the spirit." I clapped her on the back. "Now go kick some baker butt."

"What are you going to do?" Emily asked, looking from me to Albus.

"We'll spectate, of course." I glanced down at my familiar. "And Albus will undoubtedly try to steal the crumbs."

Emily snickered. "I wouldn't have it any other way."

CHAPTER THREE

"Well, that could have gone better." Albus trotted alongside me while we looked for a place to sit. A grassy hill overlooked the bakers' stations and provided ample room for spectators, not to mention a great view.

"Tell me about it," I groaned. I picked out a spot where we could see all four stations and reached into my bag, pulling out a folded blanket. "Here looks good, right Albus?"

"As good as any." He sniffed the grass and gingerly stepped onto the blanket. When I sat down, he curled up in my lap. "I was really hoping to get some behind the scenes action, though."

"Oh, Albus." I scratched him behind the ears and stared off at the clouds. "They wouldn't have let you in the kitchens anyway."

"Excuse me!" He tilted his head upward, glaring like I'd called him fat.

"What?" I shrugged. "I know you're careful, but they have a no animals rule. Even for witches. The health department could shut them down, and being that they're mostly human, it's better if they stay out of it."

"But I thought the witches set up a barrier around the festival grounds so no humans would stumble upon it anyway?" Albus lay his head on his paws and stared off into the distance at the bakers setting up their stations. "And besides, since when do you care so much about rules? That's not the Kat I know. You never care about them when you're trying to solve a mystery, for example."

"That's different!" I scowled.

"How?" Albus shot back.

"It just..." I stammered. "It just is!" The answer was so obvious, I couldn't even articulate it. Apparently.

Albus: 1. Kat: 0.

The sound of a horn cut off our bickering and drew our attention to the podium. A lady with platinum blonde hair in tight curls and glasses on a chain stepped up to the mic.

"Welcome, ladies, and gentlemen, to the Harvest Baking Championship! Here we have four of the southeast's most accomplished kitchen witches. But it wasn't easy for them to get here, oh no. They've each worked incredibly hard to beat out dozens of other applicants for a chance to be here. So let's give them a big, magical round of applause!"

I cheered and clapped for Emily, who had taken her spot at the station right up front, next to the judging table. A scattering of other spectators, friends, and family clapped and shouted their appreciation. When the noise died down, the lady at the mic spoke again.

"My name is Elmira Elderberry, and I'll be your Harvest Host here today. Joining me on the judges' panel will be three of the most distinguished bakers in the field — and here they come now!"

The judges walked up to the stage from a small tent at the back of the set, waving and smiling to the bakers and the crowd. One of them, I noticed, was the man Emily and Meryl had been fawning over — Fabio.

"He doesn't even have long, flowing hair," Albus groused when they introduced him. "He doesn't look like a Fabio at all."

"Shh," I hissed, but I couldn't hold back a snort of laughter. "How do you even know who that Fabio is — you know what, never mind!"

Albus snickered to himself as the other two

judges introduced themselves. They didn't have the same glitz and glamor aura that Fabio did, but their credentials and serious expressions more than made up for it.

"We have the prestigious Crown Hotel's chief kitchen witch joining us here today—let's give it up for Carol Doons!"

If there was a chef 'look', she had it. Well pressed coat, tight bun, not one hair out of place. She crossed her arms and looked out at the contestants before taking her seat at the judges' table.

"She must be the tough one," Albus observed.

"And last, but certainly not least, we have the editor of Kitchen Witch Weekly — Victor Halloway, all the way from New York City!"

I didn't even follow cooking, but even I had heard that name. I clapped and cheered with the rest of them. Victor, a tall, thin man with gray hair and glasses, took his seat between Fabio and Carol. They waved and gave their best showtime smiles.

The only thing left now was to introduce the contestants, and the event could begin.

"Now, bakers — each one of you will be assigned a specific dessert for this competition. You will have to create this dessert based on a set of given parameters. This is not your grandmother's cooking competition. And what would the Harvest Baking

Championship be without a little magic? You will each be required to display a magical effect in your presentation. What those desserts and effects are, as well as what ingredients you will be using, is up to these."

She stepped aside and revealed eight glass jars on the table next to her. From this distance, I could see they were full of something, but of what?

"Within these jars are slips of paper containing different dishes and different spells. Take one gold and one silver jar, and prepare to wow the judges. You have sixty minutes. Bakers, are you ready?"

They nodded.

"Then the Harvest Baking Championship will begin in 3...2...1...Go!" She blew a whistle and got out of dodge. All four bakers sprinted for the jars. Some of them nearly tumbled over one another, but not Emily. She dodged and weaved with ease, grabbing her selections first and rushing back to her station.

When the dust settled, each of them wrote up on a large whiteboard their assignments so that the judges and the audience could see.

Tense music pumped in the background as they worked, and I held my breath waiting for the announcement.

Emily's swirly handwriting finally showed up on

the whiteboard. That's when I knew she had this in the bag.

Sweet treat: Donuts.

Magic effect: color — wow us with your use of sparkle and flair. Let us actually *taste the rainbow!*

I glanced at Albus and pointed. There couldn't have been a more perfect challenge. Emily's donuts were legend. Everyone in town said so. And on top of that, she never shied away from trying new flavors or ingredients. Once, for Grandma Crystal's birthday, she'd made a cake that literally shot off fireworks. Magical fireworks, of course, but oh, what a display it was!

"She's totally got this." I grinned and looked at Albus. "Donuts are Emily's specialty."

"That may be," Albus observed, "but we don't know how well the others fit with their selections. They may be just as aligned."

I tapped my chin. "True. But remember that fireworks cake she made for Grandma Crystal last year? That was epic."

"And I'm sure she'll come up with something just as great. She's got a creative head on her shoulders. Just hope she can make do without her grimoire."

My stomach sunk, the sense of joy I had only moments earlier already vanishing. Right. Kitchen witches relied on grimoires more than the rest of us — they held the whole of a witches' knowledge and experience. And for a kitchen witch, the purpose was twofold. It served not only as a repository for magical knowledge but the applications of that work to the world of cooking as well. A cookbook of the most magical sort, you could say.

But this time, Emily wouldn't have it by her side.

"She'll be fine," I said. Each of the other teams was already hard at work. Each of them already had large, glowing volumes open on the desk.

Would she even have a chance?

I sucked in a breath and shook my head. There wasn't any sense in entertaining that thought. I believed in Emily, more so than even she did sometimes. And I knew one thing for sure: she hadn't come this far just to give up now.

"Come on, Emily!" I whooped. She whipped her head to the source of the sound and waved, a grin stretching across her face. "You can do it!"

Emily pumped her fist into the air in response, sparks flying from her fingertips. "For Haven!" She cried.

"For Haven!" I cheered in response.

Albus meowed and leaped off my lap, clearly upset I was bouncing around so much.

"Meow!" He yelped, looking down at the bakers.

Close enough.

About ten minutes into the bake, before the air started to smell with the delicious aromas of autumn, the sound of a gong rang out across the field.

We all looked up to see what was going on. The host walked out of the tent once more, a smug smile on her face.

"Oh, bakers!" She addressed the frantic contestants as if she had all the time in the world. "One more thing, to make the game a little more interesting. You see, each of the jars we actually enchanted to provide you with your signature dish and presentation style. That's right — each of you received the dessert and the spell you're most proficient at. But there's a twist — that's not the dish you'll be making today."

My eyes widened. The bakers, still working tirelessly, stopped and stuttered for a moment, glancing at one another.

"That's right..." Elmira announced. "Bakers, put your hands up. Step away from your stations. For this twist, each baker will move one station clockwise, and *that* will be your assignment for this competition. Good luck."

I gasped. A fraction of a second of silence fell over the valley as the news sank in. But there was no time to protest. No time to think of a new plan. The bakers had to move. Emily left her donuts and her glittery display behind, moving clockwise to Meryl's station. Each of the bakers, looking crestfallen, to say the least, moved to the next station in line.

Now each of them, instead of baking something they loved and excelled at, had to create someone else's specialty.

In even less time.

CHAPTER FOUR

My heart went out to the bakers. I knew these competitions never made it easy, but this was ridiculous. To have skill and certainty ripped away from you like that...

I guess it tested more than just a witch's cooking skills. The ability to think on their feet and their ability to adapt also came in handy.

"Well *now* what?" Albus asked, staring at the scene just as intently as I was. "What did she get instead? I can't see."

I squinted to find the whiteboard on Emily's new station. Everyone rushed about and the floor was filled with panicked muttering, but I caught sight of the assignment.

"Pumpkin pie."

"That's what that other girl had? Not a bad choice. I could really go for a pumpkin pie right now, to be honest..."

I eyed him. "Is there any time you're not thinking about food?"

He paused and licked a paw, not meeting my gaze. "Let me get back to you on that."

I rolled my eyes. Typical cat.

The bakers, considerably more confused and disheveled than before, took their places at the new stations. Their expressions ranged from annoyance to flat-out panic, and I couldn't blame them. The festival was known for its game-changing twists, but no one saw this one coming.

"Do you think she'll be all right?" Albus asked.

I nodded. "She's been through more stressful times than this. Remember when Miss Olson needed last-minute catering for her wedding?"

"I remember all the leftovers."

"What I'm saying is," I continued, ignoring his constant food references, "that she's come through in a pinch before. I'm just as excited as the rest of the audience to see how she does it."

"May the best baker win," the host's amplified voice boomed across the valley, the clock continued ticking, and the game was afoot once more.

I had to hand it to the bakers — they put out some impressive work. Each of them moved so quickly, so efficiently around their stations, I could only watch in awe. In a cynical sort of way, I was kind of glad I wasn't allowed into the competition. There was no way I could measure up to that level of skill.

While I kept an eye on everyone, I watched Emily most of all. Pumpkin pie wasn't a terribly hard dish to make, but it was easy to screw up if you didn't know what you were doing. The ratios of spices had to be just right as did the consistency of the pumpkin filling. Anything less and you'd end up with a goopy, foul-tasting mess.

Add in the magical element of the challenge and Emily had her hands full. Assigned to her station was a spell I'd scarcely seen before: message magic. Instead of a glamorous display of lights and colors, the pie would be enchanted to display a message. It could be either in words or in voice.

The only time I'd seen such magic was when I visited my Uncle Ben, a word witch and eccentric antique collector. He was more than a little bit odd and some folks found that off-putting, but not me. He was weird, but so was I. The quirkiness was endearing.

That type of magic was usually done on static objects, though. I'd never seen it used in tandem with food before.

"I hope that mean girl eats her words," Albus joked. "Get it?"

I rolled my eyes. "Haha, very funny." But it was an interesting idea — could one actually *taste* the message imbued in the pie?

The host took the podium once more, and I knew we were about to get an answer.

"Hands up, bakers!" She called brightly. Her voice rang through the valley like birdsong. Just like that, the storm of frenetic activity stopped. The bakers backed away from their stations, finally taking a breath. Each of their dishes sat on the stations before them, steaming, glowing, or in some cases, slithering.

The mixture of scents rising up toward us made my mouth water. "What do you think they do with all the leftovers?" I asked Albus. "They can't eat it all during the judging, and would be a shame to let it go to waste..."

"Way ahead of you," Albus replied, nodding toward the judge's stations. "They have a table behind the judges with storage containers for the extra food. Seems like a nice buffet if you ask me."

Elmira continued her announcements, but an eerie silence fell upon the valley. For the last hour, the kitchen positively vibrated with movement, magic, and excitement. Now the die was cast. Each baker's dessert lay on the station in front of them, and all that was left was the judging.

"I want to congratulate all of you on doing such a fine job, especially in the wake of our last-minute twist. You'll be judged on three factors: taste, presentation, and incorporation of the magical theme. Emily, you're up first. Please bring your dessert to the judges' table."

I held my breath. Emily picked up the plates of steaming pumpkin pie and brought them to the judges, a big, confident smile on her face.

Fabio, clearly the head judge, simply stared at the plate in front of him as if dissecting it with his eyes. The other two did the same, waiting for Emily's description of what they were about to eat.

"Autumn is in the air here in Haven, and I thought what better way to represent that than with a delicious pumpkin pie. I've combined the traditional pumpkin and spices together with a toasted marshmallow topping and chocolate shavings."

My stomach rumbled. It *did* look good.

"And for the magical element?" Carol asked. She poked at her slice with a small fork but didn't eat yet.

That was the real test. I'd never seen Emily use word magic, and especially without her spellbook, the chances weren't good.

"I've incorporated a bit of messaging magic to share with you today. All you need to do is pick up the fork and dig in."

The judges glanced at one another. Seemed simple enough. Fabio poked his fork into the pie and pulled off a small bite to trigger the reaction.

And what a reaction it was.

A burst of steam billowed into the air like a mushroom cloud, sweet and fragrant. Out of the steam, letters formed in midair.

I squinted to get a better look, but no, I wasn't seeing things. A cold weight of dread dropped into my stomach as I mouthed each letter.

D-I-E.

"I beg your pardon?!" Fabio shrunk back from the dish like he'd been shocked. "Did you just threaten me?"

Emily, for her part, looked just as disturbed. All

the color drained from her face, leaving a white sheet of terror. She stammered and stumbled over her words, trying to form an explanation. "I'm so sorry, sir. It was supposed to say P-I-E, pie. I swear, it wasn't intentional..."

"If I find out that it was," he interrupted, eyes narrowed. "There will be serious penalties."

"I understand, sir, but I promise the taste will more than make up for it, you'll see."

He stared at it for another long moment. "Hmm. I'll be the judge of that." The frown didn't leave his face as he popped the small bite of pie into his mouth.

I crossed my fingers and watched the scene breathlessly, praying that Emily could recover. What was she thinking, spelling out the word "die"? Even if it was a mistake, she should have been more careful. Picked some word or phrase that couldn't be so easily garbled. Threatening a judge was no small matter, and people had been dropping dead way more than I was comfortable with this year.

But that was crazy. This wasn't a murder. The judge wasn't dead. Just my imagination on overdrive. Just the stress of dealing with two murder cases in such a small period of time.

At least, that's what I thought.

Fabio's eyes grew wide. His body tensed and shook. His mouth sagged open, spittle draining down his chin. With a choked gasp, he pitched forward, face-first, into the pie.

CHAPTER FIVE

I thought the baking itself was chaos. I hadn't
seen anything yet.

From the moment Fabio face-planted in
the pumpkin pie, the entire crowd went nuts. Carol
screamed and leaped up from her chair, knocking it
over in her haste. The judge on the other side of him
leaned over and tried to pick him up. He placed a
hand to the side of his neck and within seconds,
screamed as well.

"He's dead!" Victor shrieked, and that's when all
spell broke loose.

Albus and I were already rushing toward the
scene. I didn't care that we weren't allowed down
there with the bakers. Someone just died. That made
the rules irrelevant. The entire way, though, I

couldn't help but feel the familiar dread bubbling up in my gut.

Again. Another dead body. Again.

Why did this always have to happen to me?

I reached the judges' table in a matter of seconds. Emily stood there, staring in horror at the plate of food she'd prepared.

D-I-E.

"She killed Fabio!" Someone yelped. "We all saw it!"

That was certainly what it looked like, but it couldn't be. Could it?

Emily buried herself in my arms, her eyes watering. "Kat, I swear, I didn't do it...I don't know what happened, I..."

"You killed him, is what happened." Meryl stepped in, arms crossed. "Maybe that's why you were so desperate to get into this tournament, so you'd finally have access to Fabio. So you could finally take him out." Her eyes narrowed.

"Excuse me," I growled and stepped between them. I didn't like being the mediator, but if I didn't do something they were going to start throwing punches. Or worse, spells.

"No one is accusing anyone of anything. We don't know what happened, and we don't have any proof." I spoke plainly, trying to keep them both calm, but in reality, I was the one that needed reassurance.

"Says you," Coral sneered. "Seems pretty clear to me. Fabio gets the pie. It spells out the word 'die', of all things, then the moment he takes a bite, he keels over. What's to prove about that?"

"I..." I bit my lip. Emily was my cousin and one of my best friends, but that was hard to argue with. "I just think we need to investigate this a little more before we jump to conclusions."

"And who's going to do that? You?"

That had my hackles up. Albus tensed and hissed next to me. "Why not me? I've actually helped the police solve two cases just this year."

Meryl snorted. "What are you, some kind of Nancy Drew? You're just a witch, and probably not a very good one, at that."

"How dare you—" I lunged at Meryl, but she ducked out of the way. Emily grabbed my shoulders and this time it was her holding me back, instead of the other way around.

"QUIET!"

A deep, rumbling voice shook the valley. A magical pulse flooded over us, rippling the grass and swaying the branches on the trees. Footsteps came closer.

A strange man walked toward us. With slicked-back gray hair and a mutton chop beard, he looked like an old war general. A scar ruined his left eye, leaving only one piercing green pupil. Bushy white eyebrows furrowed in confusion and shock, but even more appalling than that was the tall, gnarled staff he carried, glowing with magical light.

A *warlock* — the highest ranking magical being there was.

The crowd parted around him as he walked. Each step crunched through the grass and leaves with deadly certainty. Even Albus shrunk away and hid behind my leg.

"I came to Haven to find our missing inspector. I didn't expect this." He pulled out a card and flashed it at us too fast to read. "Kaspar Hunt, Senior Agent. The PEA is quite interested in you."

"Who, me?" Emily asked, her voice shaking.

"Are you the leader of this locality?" His words didn't spare any extra effort. They were crisp, clean. Just like the clothes he wore.

"Um, no." Emily rubbed the back of her neck.

"Then it matters not. We are more concerned with the conduct of this Haven of yours, as a whole. First, your name comes up in that werewolf business, unsolved might I add, then one of our best agents goes MIA. Coincidence? They sent me to find out.

Imagine my reaction when I get here and see that I've walked right into a crime scene."

I gulped. That did sound pretty serious.

"I can explain..." Emily started. "It was an accident, I swear..."

He raised an eyebrow. "And everyone else here, they witnessed this 'accident' as well? Just what were you all doing here?"

"The Harvest Baking Championship," Ginger spoke up for the first time. "It's a popular cooking competition between witches, something like the Olympics of food. We were here, and we were baking, and then..." She grimaced. "He just fell over, poof, right in the pie."

"Hmm." He walked forward and observed the scene. He pulled on a latex glove then stuck a finger into the offending pie, bringing a bit of it up to his nose.

"Not poison, but there's something...off about it." He frowned. "Tell me, what happened right before this fellow's untimely demise?"

All eyes turned to Emily, who shrunk away even further.

"You there, did you bake this pie?" The agent's questions were nothing if not straightforward.

"Yes, but..."

"Then I'll be needing to ask you a few questions.

All of you here, in fact. With Agent Douglas missing and this reckless use of magic...Haven's worse off than I thought." He scrubbed a hand over his face and sighed. "Party's over, people."

I tried to catch Emily's attention but Agent Hunt was already leading her away. "Wait!" I yelped, running after them. "What are you going to do with her?"

He turned and raised a condescending eyebrow. How dare someone question him, right? "And who might you be?" He drawled. "If you can't tell I'm very busy at the moment."

"Kat Sullivan," I spat the words as quickly as I could, for fear he would get tired of listening and take Emily away for good. "I can help."

"You?" The corners of his lips quirked upward. "Help me? I'm sorry miss, but this is no place for amateur sleuths. Go on home now. Don't even think about leaving. I'll be back."

"The rest of you." He turned back to the murmuring crowd and spread his arms wide. "I've got some workers coming to deal with the mess you've made, in the meantime get on back to your homes. We'll be interviewing all witnesses, so don't go far." He waved a hand with no more care than flicking a fly. "Disperse."

With that, he turned on his heel and walked

away, leaving us fuming in the dust. Alone.

CHAPTER SIX

It wasn't long until more workers swooped in — some of them quite literally — to clean up the mess. I did my best to stay out of their way, but Agent Hunt's words still rung harshly in my ears. Not to mention they had Emily.

I had a knack for making quick, sometimes reckless decisions, but even I wasn't crazy enough to go up against the PEA. They were just too powerful. If I wanted to figure this out and save my friend, I'd have to do it a different way.

Unfortunately, that way would have to wait. Agent Hunt was already clearing the area while two other tough-looking guards set up a perimeter.

I sighed and left the area, Albus at my heels. The car felt awfully empty as I drove home this time. On the way over here, Emily sat in the passenger seat, laughing and talking. Now, those awful PEA men had her, and I didn't know when I'd hear from her again. She must be terrified.

The organization had already done enough to hurt their family — imposing restrictions on her father's business, for example — and now she was literally in the belly of the beast. My stomach did flip flops in response. Even Albus didn't have the same chatty remarks he always did, and that's when you know it's a real problem.

When your snarky familiar stops snarking, things were getting serious.

The whole rest of the day I milled around the house like a zombie. I couldn't eat, I was too wired to sleep, and even Albus wasn't cheering me up. The whole thing settled on my shoulders like one of Emily's giant cast iron pans, and I couldn't shake it.

I thought about calling up my best friend Pepper, but what would I even say? "Oh, by the way, I witnessed another murder today. And how are you?"

I sunk into the couch next to Albus and pressed a pillow over my face. This was *so* not going the way

I'd hoped. Why did I offer to help with the baking championship again?

Oh yeah, cause Emily twisted my arm into it. Thanks, Emily.

Sleep descended slowly that night, even though I had my phone next to my bed with the ringer on. Just in case. I'd expected to hear from Emily, if not the agent himself, and the fact that I'd heard from neither was more than a little disheartening. What were they going to do with her?

I wasn't going to wait around to find out.

I gathered up my courage (as well as my cat) then high-tailed it across town to my best friend's house. It was the middle of the night, but that didn't matter. I'd always been there for her when she needed me. I sat up with her all night when she had food poisoning, and cried with her when her beloved dog Benny passed away. We were there for each other no matter what, and I wouldn't trade that for the world.

It took her a few sleepy minutes to answer the door. Couldn't blame her; it was just after three in the morning. But sometimes there's a problem so big you can't sit with it alone, even overnight. That's why I needed my bestie.

Pepper opened the door and rubbed her eyes. She wore a fluffy pink robe and bunny slippers. Her usually wild hair was even more so, piled into a messy bun on top of her head.

"Kat?" She mumbled sleepily. "What time is it?"

I gave her an apologetic smile. "Can I come in?"

"Yeah, sure." She held open the door for Albus and me to step in from the chill. "Don't mind the mess."

I knew my friend well enough to know she wasn't the tidiest person around, but I still cringed a little bit. I couldn't help it. Running The Curious Cauldron meant that everything had to have a place and a purpose. If something wasn't in the right place or wasn't sorted properly, it would cost even more time and money down the road to fix it.

Pepper, on the other hand, seemed to thrive in chaos.

Well, they did always say opposites attract.

Pepper trudged her way into the kitchen and flicked on a few lights. I squinted against the brightness, but it helped me wake up. "Is this a coffee or alcohol kind of story?"

She always said there were only two types of crises, and they needed very different remedies.

"Um...both?" I cracked a smile. "It's been that kind of day."

"Oh, believe me, you don't want both. Did that

once. Never again. Only time I've ever puked from drinking, and I'm not looking to repeat it." She put her hands on her hips and stared into the fridge for a moment to make up her mind. "I'll tell you what. I'm tired as a hibernating grizzly so I'm gonna fix a cup of coffee. You're welcome to one as well. Maybe it will help you think."

"Yeah," I said, still a bit shaken. "Maybe."

I slid into one of the high chairs up against her kitchen bar and rested my chin in my hands. "You sure you don't want me to get that for you? I'm the one that came barging in overnight and everything."

"Don't worry about it," Pepper said, some of the energy already returning to her voice. "What are friends for?"

Albus perched on the chair next to me, looking across the kitchen hopefully. "Do you think she forgot about me?"

"I think Albus wants something as well. Do you have any of those homemade treats left over?"

"In the pantry," Pepper pointed behind her. "It's not like I have any animals eating them at the moment."

It was a casual enough statement, but I could hear the hurt in her voice. Pepper had been gifted with the talent of animals. Where I excelled with the natural world, plants, and earth, she found a greater affinity to animals than most. That's why she helped out at the shelter in her spare time and usually fed strays roaming around the neighborhood. It was extra disheartening, then, that she had never found an animal familiar of her own.

While Albus gobbled up a handful of treats, I gratefully took the steaming cup of coffee and sat down at the raised table next to Pepper.

"So," she said over the rim of her mug, "What happened?"

Where to even start? "You know that baking competition Emily was so excited about?"

"Yeah, the Harvest thing?"

"That was yesterday. She brought me along as a helper, but they changed the rules and I couldn't join, so I stayed and watched."

"That was yesterday?" Pepper nearly spit out her overly-sugared coffee. "Shoot, I totally messed up the date. I wanted to be there to cheer her on."

"Maybe it's a good thing that you weren't." I grimaced and took another sip. The hot liquid washed away some of the panic and exhaustion, but it would take a lot more than that to get me feeling back to normal.

"Why? Someone burn their brownies or something?"

"No. Something worse." I let out a shaky breath, steeling myself for what to say next. "They each had assignments to bake a certain type of dessert. Emily got donuts — well, she did, but then they changed it up in a twist — so then she had to make a pumpkin pie. I thought she was doing all right, and it all looked really good until she brought it to the judges."

"They didn't like it?" Pepper asked. "I don't see how anyone could dislike her food. It's the best."

"You...could say that." Even now, the letters D-I-E flickered like ghosts before my eyes. "When the head judge ate a piece of the pie, he started getting all weird, and then he..." My voice broke. "I don't get it, Pepper. He's dead."

This time she really did choke. I had to clap her on the back to get her breathing again. When Pepper regained her composure and wiped her watering eyes, she asked the question we'd all been wondering.

"I'm sorry, what? Next time you gotta tell me something like that, wait till I'm not drinking!"

"I wouldn't believe it either, but I saw it with my own eyes."

Pepper looked even more worried if that were possible. "Kat, seriously. What is it with you and dead bodies lately? Are you cursed?"

I laughed it off, but part of it rang a little too

true for comfort. "I guess I keep ending up at the wrong place at the wrong time." I shrugged. "I'm getting pretty tired of it too. And this time it's personal."

"They don't think Emily actually did it, do they? They're crazy — she wouldn't hurt a fly!"

"That's not even the worst of it." I ran a hand through Albus' fur for comfort. "Cooper's not even involved this time. The regular Haven police are none the wiser, best I can tell. The PEA themselves arrived just as it happened. Pep, they brought an actual *warlock*."

"No way," she breathed, her eyes large as our saucers. "I've never seen one in real life before."

"He was very intimidating. And kind of a jerk."

"Figures. But why was he here in the first place?"

"Remember the last time I found a dead guy?" Yeah, saying that would never not feel weird.

"Oh man...you're right. That guy was from the PEA too, wasn't he?"

"Yup, and I can bet you money the PEA wasn't too thrilled when he didn't return."

"Understandable. So they sent in the big guns."

"That's what it looks like." I sighed. "And then we made Haven look even worse. They just came here to find Ian, and then to stumble across yet another dead body...it's no wonder they're conducting a full investigation after what happened with Mayor Armstrong, too."

Pepper buried her head in her hands, hair falling around her shoulders in messy waves. "When did Haven get so crazy? This isn't the town I knew. Remember back when I moved here? Everything was so...normal."

I scoffed. "That's because you hadn't gotten to know all of us weirdos yet."

"Who are you calling a weirdo?" Albus yelped from under the table.

"The point is," I pushed back my mug and gave her a serious look. "Emily is in danger. Haven is in danger. I can't just sit around and let this happen, Pep. I want to do something, but I don't know what."

Pepper chewed her lip for a moment in thought. She fiddled with her robe and hair, not meeting my eyes. "I know you don't want to hear this, Kat, but I really don't think getting involved right now is a good idea. You said yourself the PEA have their eyes peeled for anything unusual. They're just looking for reasons to bring in new rules, new restrictions, new leaders. I'm not as crazy as Mayor Armstrong, but he did have a point under all the bigotry and brainwashing. Haven is...well, a haven. For all of us. And having the PEA here only threatens that."

I scowled. Why did she have to be right? I hated

when she was right — especially when that meant I was wrong.

There was no denying the truth, though. Haven was definitely in hot water, and with it, all the residents as well.

"Just please," Pepper begged me, her eyes wide. "Sit this one out. Focus on The Curious Cauldron. Focus on what you can control. This will blow over, but we have to keep our noses clean."

"Like she's ever been able to stay out of it before," Albus snarked. Good thing Pepper couldn't hear him — I'm sure she'd have a thing or two to say about my mouthy cat as well.

Exhaustion and frustration in equal measure flooded over me. I came over here for a helping hand. For a supportive shoulder. And that she was — but instead of making me feel better, I only felt more powerless.

More unable to save Emily or Haven itself for that matter.

With that thought weighing heavy on my soul, I excused myself, thanked her for the coffee, and headed back to my car.

Pepper was only looking out for me. I knew that.

Then why was it so hard to accept?

I rested my head against the steering wheel and looked over at Albus. "What do you think?"

"Since when do you ever listen to me?"

"Albus," I groaned. "Not now. I'm seriously asking you."

"Well, apparently you're a naughty little rule-breaker now, so no sense in stopping at this point."

Another groan. Guess he had a point.

CHAPTER SEVEN

I managed to get an entire hour of sleep before my alarm went off. My feet trudged across the floor and the bags under my eyes were so large they'd have to go in oversized luggage.

I thought about taking the day off — I could make the rules, it was my shop after all — but thought better of it. I couldn't take a day off every time I didn't feel up to it, and besides, my customers depended on me.

Not to mention the work of fulfilling orders and interacting with customers would give me something to do. Something to occupy me so I didn't keep replaying the incident.

I checked my phone for about the hundredth time. Nope. Still no word from Emily or the agent. I thought about calling Emily's phone, but knowing them they probably confiscated it or something.

"What are you doing?" Albus peered up at me, eyes half-open. "I was sleeping. You should try it sometime."

"I was just checking to see if I missed anything from Emily."

"Kat." Oh no, there was the Mr. Important Familiar voice. "How many times have you checked that thing? Am I going to have to hide it again?"

"No —" I froze. "Wait, that was *you*?"

Albus bolted the split second before I lunged at him.

The cell phone buzzed in my hand and I wasted no time smashing the answer button. "Hello? Emily? Is that you?"

"Well, hello to you too, Miss Sullivan. This is Kaspar Hunt from the PEA. I'm calling about the incident you witnessed."

"Oh." I deflated, sinking into a nearby chair. "Right." Albus was nowhere nearby. For once, I actually wanted the little pest here to keep me centered.

"Go ahead, out with it. What do you want?" I didn't have time or energy to play games today, and my nerves were still on edge.

"I'm interviewing each of the witnesses separately at the scene. You'll need to answer a few questions but it shouldn't take too long. Are you free?"

I pressed the area between my brows where a headache already started to pound. "Do I have to come in immediately?"

"That would be ideal, yes."

I clenched my jaw. So far, I was zero for two on good experiences with the PEA. Were they all like this?

"I have to work this morning," I told him through gritted teeth.

"I know." His voice remained as chipper as ever. "But our records indicate that as a business owner, you can open and close the shop at will, correct?"

My mouth dropped open. "I, uh..."

"I'll see you at the clearing in half an hour. Goodbye."

With a newfound understanding of Mayor Armstrong's frustration, I dropped everything and drove over to the fairgrounds.

I'd only ever worked with the PEA through mail as a young adult when I applied for my witch's license. That was a pain in the rear enough to not want to repeat it, but this was something else entirely.

Albus begged to stay home and sleep, so I crawled out of the car alone, approaching the scene for the second time.

In some ways, it looked the same as I had left it. Four cooking stations. A judges' table. A tent for the staff and equipment. But this time as I approached, it was all strangely...sanitized.

Yellow tape surrounded the perimeter and there were signs and markings on the ground in a few spots — I assumed those were clues or extra areas they meant to investigate.

The magical barrier that surrounded the valley still held firm. Whoever put it up knew what they were doing. When I stepped through it was only a small tickle, but should someone without magical powers approach, they'd find themselves faced with an illusion of an empty field. That, and a strong desire to stay away.

I spotted a second figure beside the inspector as I neared the scene. A smaller, slighter figure heading toward me, instead of away.

When she got close enough I realized it was Coral, one of the bakers from the competition. It made sense — Agent Hunt said he was interviewing everyone. Guess she'd just finished up.

"Hey there." I threw up a hand in greeting. "Coral, right?"

"Yeah. He call you in too?"

"He did." I nodded. "How bad was it?"

She snorted. "See for yourself. I had to extend my stay because of this madness."

"Oh, where are you staying? I know a couple of the people that work around town, I could pull some strings to get you a discount — as apologies for the inconvenience."

Rule number one of interviewing suspects: always give them something first. Make them think you're on their side.

Coral gaped at me quizzically. "Why?" She said at last. "It's not your fault...is it?" Her voice lowered on the last words, making the hairs on the back of my neck stand up.

"What? No." I shook my head frantically. "That's not what I meant. It's just that I know how tough it can be, stranded in a strange place. And we here in Haven try to look out for one another. Guests included."

Coral still looked skeptical, but her expression softened. "You really don't have to do anything, but..."

"But...?"

"If you really want to help, go over to The

Starlight Bed and Breakfast. The other two bakers are there too if you're curious. They were up partying half the night. Couldn't sleep a wink." With an exaggerated yawn, Coral sidestepped me. "I'm going to go take a nap. Good luck out there...oh, I'm sorry, I can't remember your name."

"Kat," I called after her. "And thanks."

"Later!" She threw up a hand in farewell, already walking away.

"So," I muttered to myself. "I know where they're staying. And with them practically stuck here in Haven..." My thoughts trailed off.

If I was going to do the amateur sleuth thing and start talking to the suspects — not that I would *ever* do something like that — I knew now where to find them.

Agent Kaspar Hunt stood in the middle of it all, just as intimidating as ever. He wore the same elegant garb I'd seen before — had he slept? — and his staff rested by his side, glowing faintly.

"Interesting spell, that." He pointed to the barely visible barrier around us. "Who cast it?"

"I don't know," I said honestly. "It's a neat trick, though." He didn't seem to be a man known for building rapport, so I didn't know why he was making small talk. I indulged him, for the moment.

"We could use something like that back at HQ."

He tapped his chin in thought. "I would love to speak to the witch who did it."

"Well, if I find out, you'll be the first to know." I gave him the biggest smile I could, but it was faker than a three dollar bill. "Now are we going to stand around chit-chatting all day? I thought you had some questions for me." I stood my ground and narrowed my eyes. "Surely you with your detailed 'records' must know I have a very busy life to get back to."

A muscle in Agent Hunt's jaw twitched. "Do not get smart with me, Miss Sullivan." He took a step forward till I was in his shadow. "I have the power to recommend your suspension. Remember that."

I gulped, but my resolve didn't waver. I hated being pushed around more than anything, but sometimes I got a little *too* passionate about it.

Cool it, Kat. I reminded myself. *Cool it. This guy's not worth it.*

"If you're ready," he said in a tone dripping with condescension. "We can begin." He waved his staff and a notepad appeared next to him, floating in midair. A pen hovered over the page at the ready.

"I hope you don't mind if I take a few notes." He tilted his head toward the notebook.

I didn't appreciate him treating me like a child, but what could I really do?

"Now *that's* a neat trick." I pointed at the floating

pen and paper. "Does it take down everything we say?"

"See for yourself."

With a flick of his hand, the pages turned toward me. Sure enough, our entire conversation was there, accurate to the letter. "Handy," I admitted.

And a good way to twist my words out of context.

Most of the questions were pretty generic. Where was I, what did I see, what happened first, what happened next. But as the time wore on, he delved deeper and with less and less relation to the case at hand.

"Do you know anything regarding the whereabouts of Ian Douglas? He was last seen here in Haven, then we lost comms. He's part of the reason I'm here."

The snarky part of my brain wanted to protest. Shouldn't they *know* where their own people were if they could track us so easily? I thought better of it, though, and didn't say a word.

"I saw him when he first came to town. That's about it." I held my breath and waited for his reaction. What if he could detect lies too?

"Very well." He said, pacing toward one of the

stations. He picked at a bit of lint on his suit and flicked it away. "I assume you know what he was looking for." It wasn't a question.

My blood ran cold. Ian's arrival had heralded a whole new chain of events, some of which I never could have expected.

"A werewolf." I tried my best to sound casual. "Did he ever find the rogue?"

Agent Hunt eyed me so fiercely I thought his gaze would pierce right through my skull. "You tell me."

My heart stuttered, thumping loudly against my chest. One of the shocking revelations I'd had was that a secret family of werewolves lived right here in Haven.

Oh yeah, and my crush Chance Wilder was one of them.

They had their own stories to tell, though. *These aren't the wolves you're looking for*. Unlike the werewolves of legend, they'd learned to work with their condition and control it enough to be around others peacefully.

My stomach sank as I remembered something else. It was only because of Ian's childhood with Chance that they were hidden from the PEA. With Ian gone...I shivered. Would they be next in the PEA's watchful eye?

"I've told you all I know." It came out a little less certain than I'd hoped, but I managed not to wince.

"Very well," Agent Hunt said again. He motioned to his floating notebook, which ticked something off with a flourish. "Do know that any information you can give us about unregistered paranormals in the area would be most..." His lips twisted into a menacing grin. "Appreciated."

I nodded and held my ground, even though every cell in my body screamed to run. "Understood." I looked around at the scene once more. Empty. Desolate. Not to mention a little creepy, knowing what had happened here so recently. A breeze pricked up goosebumps on my arms and I hugged myself. "Am I free to go?"

He looked me up and down. As much as he wanted to keep me around and interrogate me further, my work here was done. He threw his head to the side and spat. With a loud thump of his staff, he waved me away.

"One more thing," I said, knowing full well I was pushing my luck. "Where's Emily?"

He blinked, expressionless. "I'm sorry, who?"

I clenched my hands into fists and let out a breath through my nose. "Emily Morris. My cousin. You drug her away from the scene and I haven't seen her since."

"I see." Agent Hunt shrugged, stoking my fury even higher. "I'm not at liberty to discuss that information. I suggest you leave before you meet the same fate."

Was he threatening me now?

As much as I wanted to let him have it, I backed away, blood still pounding in my ears.

"Don't even think about leaving town." His voice echoed after me. "This case is far from over."

And that's just what I was afraid of.

CHAPTER EIGHT

With more questions than answers, I dragged myself to The Curious Cauldron and opened up shop for the day. If there was one thing that always kept me going, it was the smiles on my customers' faces.

That, and having something to do with my hands so that my mind didn't run away with me.

Grandma Crystal told stories of how she coped after her husband's death. It was work, she said, that had saved her. Work doesn't care who you are or what you've been through. You either show up or you don't.

Some people thought that was a bit too cold, but right now it suited me just fine. If I let every emotion and fear about this situation worm its way in, I'd be in a quivering ball in the corner.

And believe me, that's never a good look.

I hunched over the smoking cauldron. Beads of sweat gathered on my forehead, threatening to trickle into my eyes. I blinked and focused on the vial in my left hand. Too many drops of this stuff and the whole thing would blow sky high. Ask me how I know.

The concoction was a potion for one of my repeat customers, a lovely old lady named Nina. I tipped the pink liquid ever so slightly into the mix, holding my breath as the color changed from neon green to pink to finally clear.

Finally able to breathe, I set the vial aside and stirred the mixture with a reinforced steel ladle. Accidentally melting your utensils was a real job hazard in potion-making. After going through three in two months, I handed mine over to a local metal witch.

I should have done that from the beginning.

The mixture thickened and gave off a faint floral aroma — the telltale sign it was ready. Setting the ladle aside, I grabbed a delicate glass vial and dipped it into the potion, filling it to the brim. Air bubbles danced and sparkled in the potion. They reflected the light and threw rainbows across my workspace.

Last, but certainly not least, was the wax seal to finish it off. I popped in a homemade cork, willing it to expand and seal completely.

A bowl of deep red wax sat to my right, kept melted by a flame underneath. Being careful not to upset the potion, I dipped the opening into the wax and covered it.

Once it had a rustic red seal, I set it aside to cool and leaned back in my chair, finally taking a breath of relief.

Finishing a potion always felt good, but especially one as complex as this. Maybe I could rest my eyes a bit. Since no one else was in the store right now, no one would notice...

Buzz, buzz!

What was that? My eyes popped open and I lost my balance. How long had I been asleep? The chair toppled backward as my arms flailed for purchase. My butt and elbow banged against the hard floor, pain shooting up my left arm. A pile of carefully organized books wobbled precariously.

"No, no no no!" I scrambled to my feet, limbs tangled. Too late. The stack of leather-bound volumes rained on top of me like an avalanche.

Ow.

My head throbbed. My ankle ached. Not to mention I was pretty sure I bruised my tailbone.

Good thing there weren't any customers, I thought wearily. This would be a pretty awkward situation to get caught in.

Buzz buzz!

And yet, the darn thing kept ringing.

That had to be Emily!

I slapped my hand on top of the desk and fumbled for the phone without getting up. "Hello?" I mumbled. "Emily?"

In my haste, I'd forgotten to check the caller ID again.

"Everything okay, Kat? Had me worried there for a second."

Oh bones, that was Chance! "Speak for yourself. Where are you? Are you and the family okay?" I grunted, trying to get into a better position. The back of the chair still poked into my ribs.

"I could ask you the same question, you don't sound so well."

That was Chance, dodging as usual. "I was just in the middle of something at the shop. No big deal." I peeled a fallen almanac off my leg and pulled myself up. "Now stop stalling. What's up?"

"I'm..." His voice dropped, losing the confident edge it normally had. "We're..." He paused. "Well, I'm sure you know who's in town."

"You mean the PEA?" I had enough trouble with

them, and I hadn't even done anything wrong. Chance and the Wilders on the other hand were basically fugitives.

"Yup."

I swallowed the lump in my throat and righted the chair so I could sit down. One hand pressed the phone to my ear while the other cupped my chin. Obviously, I was worried about him, but I didn't know how to say that without it sounding super lame.

It was only because of their childhood friend Ian that they'd been safe this long, and now Ian was dead.

"What are you going to do?" I asked at last, almost fearing the answer.

"Same thing we always do," he said simply. "Keep our heads down. Keep our eyes and ears open. Still trying to gauge how serious of a threat we're dealing with, but if you know anything that might help..."

The interview with Agent Hunt came back to me. "I just talked to one of them. He was asking a bunch of questions, mostly about the incident at the Harvest Baking Championship, but then he started asking about wolves, too."

I could practically hear him tense up over the phone.

Chance cursed. "They're really bringing in the big boys, aren't they?"

"I guess so." I grimaced.

"Say," he interrupted my next idea. "Who all was at that Harvest thing again? Maybe my brothers and I know something that can help."

"That would be great." Chance and his guys had always worked by their own rules, but when it gave me access to inside information? Totally worth it. "Let me see if I can remember the other bakers off the top of my head..."

The first one that came to mind was Meryl. I had the most direct interaction with her so far, which wasn't saying much, but she'd left a bad taste in my mouth. If I were going on personality alone, she'd be suspect number one.

"There was this one woman named Meryl there. Supposedly some kind of hotshot. She was about as full of herself as Starla was — really rude to Emily and me when we were there."

"Meryl..." he thought for a moment. "Meryl Mason?"

That sounded familiar. "Yeah, I think so."

"It's unlikely it's the same person, but let's just say that name's come up in some of the...shadier communities of late."

A chill ran down my spine. "Like criminals, or...?"

"That's not important." He brushed the question off too quickly, but don't think I didn't notice. "But she's been into some pretty weird stuff lately. I wouldn't trust her as far as I can throw her."

Yup, that sounded like the Meryl I knew. "Okay. Thanks." My shoulders slumped with the weight of the day. I picked up my empty coffee mug for the fifth time, trying to will it to refill itself.

I should have been a coffee witch.

"This whole thing just has me so nervous," I admitted. "And I'm sure it's not been easy for you either."

"I'm managing." His short, clipped sentences didn't inspire a lot of confidence though.

"The thing is, they're not just here about the Ian thing or the Harvest thing. I doubt they even know what happened with Quentin and them." I shook my head, letting the full weight of the situation dawn on me for the first time. "They're trying to do a whole inspection of the town. A full audit." The hand not holding my phone clenched into a fist. My fingernails dug into my palms.

"Making sure we're all good little witches." I spat the words like they were poison.

"So, to put it bluntly," Chance replied, no less excited, "making sure we're all under their thumb."

"Something like that." I sighed.

"Haven doesn't want to give us a break, does it?" A few voices echoed in the background. Footsteps. A door clicked closed.

Chance lowered his voice and the ambient noise faded away. "You know what will happen if the PEA catches us, Kat."

To be honest, I didn't have a full idea, but I had enough of one to scare me.

"Are you going to be okay?" My voice shook despite myself.

"Aren't we always?" I could see his self-confident smile in my mind, but it didn't show in his voice.

"Just..." I grasped for words. Nothing I could say would really change the situation, but I hated feeling so powerless. "Let me know if there's anything I can do." I bit my lip and added, "I wish you were here."

I blushed at that last part. Probably shouldn't have said that, but my nerves were so raw my filter was all but gone.

"Wish you were here too, Kitty Kat." Even though he was far away, knowing that he was thinking about me warmed my heart. "I don't think I have to tell you this, but please. Don't go getting yourself in trouble. Stay out of this. The stakes are too high, for all of us."

I huffed out an annoyed breath. Of all people, he should understand. I knew things were balanced on a knives' edge right now but did they really expect me to sit back and do *nothing*?

That's not the kind of witch I was.

I wasn't going to let this get to me though. Not today. I went with a joke instead — a natural deflection. "Look who's talking. I learned all my rule-breaking ways from the best." With a chuckle, I added, "And here I thought you would have some kind of slick plan."

"Not that you know of, anyway." There was the spirited, sarcastic Chance I'd come to know. "I gotta go, but I'll be in touch. Thanks for filling me in."

"Okay," I said breathlessly. There was so much else I wanted to say. So much more I wanted to ask him. But now wasn't the right time, and with the way things were going, that time might never come.

"Bye."

"Bye, Kat."

The call ended, and the quiet pressed in around me.

CHAPTER NINE

One thing was for certain: there was never a dull day at The Curious Cauldron. My hands and work kept me busy, leaving little time to think about much else. I was grateful for the constant flow of customers, though — it provided not only much-needed revenue but the distraction I craved.

Chance's words still rang in my head while I closed up shop for the day. I worried about him and his family out there and vulnerable, but there wasn't anything I could do. Besides, they'd made it this long without arousing suspicion. They could do it again.

Even though he told me to stay out of it, his comments about Meryl intrigued me.

If she was part of shady dealings before the tournament even started, who was to say she wouldn't do something else to clinch the title? I wanted to have a talk with her, but I knew that wasn't going to be easy.

Meryl was easily the rudest out of the three other contestants, and I highly doubted she'd welcome me in with open arms.

That's when I remembered that today was Friday. Every Friday, the Starlight Bed and Breakfast held a grand dinner for the guests. Everyone was invited to come out, enjoy the meal, and experience the best hospitality Haven had to offer.

Thanks to running into Ginger on the way to meet with Agent Hunt, I learned that she and the other bakers were staying at said Bed and Breakfast. Why not pose as part of the feast and get to know them a little better?

On the way home, I put my phone on Bluetooth and dialed up Ronnie the innkeeper. He owed me a favor and now was the perfect time to cash in.

"Hey Ronnie," I said as soon as his voice came on the line. "You still having the grand dinner tonight?"

"Yup. Every Friday. We're makin' it extra special — haven't had so many out of town visitors in so long."

"Excellent." My mind jumped ahead, already planning the next steps. "You need any help tonight?

I got some free time and I wanted to bring something over. My own little contribution as a welcome gift."

"Well..." He wheedled for a moment. "I don't see why not. But ye'll need to get here soon. We're settin' up early tonight."

"I'll be right there," I told him. "Just let me go home and change and check on Albus."

"And Kat..." Ronnie's voice trailed off. "What *happened* over there? The whole town's gone nuts."

I frowned and tapped the steering wheel. "I'll tell you as much as I can," I managed. "Let me get home and get ready. I'll see you soon."

"All right, Kat. Be careful out there."

As soon as I pulled into my driveway, I banged my head onto the steering wheel in frustration. A little too hard, unfortunately, cause the horn blared angrily from the contact.

My neighbor raised the blinds and leaned out the window to give me the stink eye.

Like I really needed that after the day I'd just had.

With a sigh, I got out of the car and unlocked the front door, already planning what I'd need to do next.

Albus, of course, shot toward me like a bullet the moment the door cracked open. "Kat! Oh, Kat! Where *were* you? I was here by myself *all day*!"

I rolled my eyes and took off my coat before stepping into the kitchen. "And?" This was a game we played every day.

"And I missed you!" Albus hopped up on the counter and followed me. "I thought we were a team. Dos amigos. Witch and familiar. Peanut butter and —"

"I get it, I get it." I laughed and scratched behind his ears, pulling him close for a hug. "It's just that you were so sleepy this morning I didn't want to disturb you. Unlike me, you didn't *have* to be at work."

"Maybe I wanted to be." He pouted with those huge round eyes, but I knew him well enough by now not to buy it. "What crazy antics did I miss this time? You didn't find any more dead bodies, did you?"

"What? No." I shivered. "Why would you even think that?"

"You've developed quite a knack for it lately if I do say so myself."

"Ugh, you and everyone else." I pulled a boxed cherry pie out of the freezer and set it on the counter to thaw. After that, I reached into the pantry and pulled out four servings of my homemade soothing serum. They were hot sellers at my shop, and with all the drama in Haven lately, they'd make nice gifts.

Setting the vials next to the pie, I headed down the hall to the bedroom. Albus, of course, didn't give up that easily.

He asked question after question while I dug through my closet. After a few minutes, I started tuning him out. Just don't tell him I said that. With a ruffled cashmere sweater and a new pair of black denim jeans, I slipped a gold necklace with an emerald pendant around my neck and checked my hair in the mirror.

"How do I look?" I said it more to myself than Albus, but he couldn't pass up a chance to make a remark.

"Like you're going on a hot date."

I snorted. "Not quite. You know the Starlight? I'm joining them for their grand dinner tonight."

"What's the occasion?"

"The other bakers from the Harvest Championship are staying there, and I thought I'd drop in to say hi — oh, and I'm not going empty-handed. People are always more friendly when you bring food."

"Let me guess," Albus drawled. "You're investigating again."

I huffed. "Is it that obvious?"

"To anyone with a pulse, yes. You don't know how to listen, do you?"

"Albus...come on. Work with me here. You know how close Emily and I are. She's family. If there's something I can do to clear her name, why wouldn't I?"

"Oh, I can think of a few reasons... but I know how you get your mind set on something. It's what drew me to you at the start if you believe it. Even if it does drive me batty at times."

I snorted and gave him a quick pet. "The feeling is mutual. Now come on, I heard they have those jelly donuts you like!"

"Kat and Albus, off on another adventure!"

The Starlight Bed and Breakfast was an old Victorian mansion in the center of town. Standing four floors tall and with plenty of rooms, hallways, and hidden alcoves to get lost in, it was a popular place for tourists and locals alike.

Rumors swirled that the place was haunted, but no one had been able to prove it. No one from the human community, that is.

Ronnie the innkeeper knew all the local ghosts, being a medium. According to him, a friendly fellow named Nigel lived in the pipes and liked to play pranks on the guests.

It all added to the charm of the place, I supposed. And it kept people coming back, which meant more business for us.

Win-win. More of a triple win, actually, once you counted that the ghosts got some fun out of it too.

Haven was a weird place sometimes, but it was my home.

I arrived at the Starlight right at six o' clock. I parked on the street and grabbed my bag from the passenger seat. Albus leaped out and followed me to the door.

I didn't even have to knock. The door opened as if by magic (spoiler: it was). The first face I saw was Ronnie, the smiling innkeeper. A stout man in his fifties, he loved nothing more than laughter and a good meal. If the sounds of merriment coming from the dining room were any indication, he was enjoying both tonight.

Ronnie outstretched his arms and welcomed me. I set the bag aside on the front reception counter and took off my coat, which he was kind enough to hang up for me.

He even snuck Albus a treat from behind the desk when he thought I wasn't looking.

When all that was done, he pulled me into a great bear hug that squeezed the air out of my lungs.

"Ron...can't breathe..."

He let up and stood back with a grin as big as his heart. "Ah, ya know I get a bit excited sometimes. It's just so good to see ya. Been a long time. Too long."

"I know," I agreed. "That's why I had to drop by. Your place is the talk of the town." Flattery would get you everywhere.

"Is that so?" He beamed rubbed his ample stomach. "Haven's bursting at the seams, she is. Not to mention this old place. But all's good in business, aye?"

"You're right about that." I'd had an uptick in business from the tourists too. I couldn't complain.

I peered past him into the dining room. The long table was already filled with faces new and old. "I'm not late, am I?"

"Just in time. Was about ta start bringing out the dishes right as ya walked in."

"Need any help with that?"

"Nah, go have a seat. And leave that pie with me."

"Sure you're not going to eat it first?" I snarked.

Ronnie laughed his way back into the kitchen. "Would I do that?" His voice echoed till the swinging kitchen door closed behind him.

Yes. Yes, he definitely would.

CHAPTER TEN

I kept the bag of free samples from my shop close at hand before stepping into the dining room. I acted as casual as possible, scouting out the final empty seat at the far end of the table.

There were more than a few faces I didn't recognize, but that wasn't why I was here.

Ginger and Coral, two of the bakers from the contest, sat across from me. Meryl, the third and final baker beside Emily, was nowhere to be found.

Which was a real shame, because I wanted to talk to her the most.

"Kat, right?" Ginger extended a hand across the table.

I nodded. "Yes, that's me. How are you enjoying Haven so far?"

"It's a lovely town," she said. "Quaint, but in a good way."

"Kind of boring, if you ask me," Coral interjected.

That stopped me mid-sentence. Sure, Haven had nothing on the bigger cities, but usually, people didn't come out and say it.

"Well, I like it." It came out as no more than a defensive mumble. Not the best look when I was trying to gain their trust.

Albus pressed a warning paw into my shoe. That was enough to reconsider my approach. "I brought you something." I pulled up the bag from beside my chair and reached inside, pulling out two small silver vials. "It's a tincture from my shop, The Curious Cauldron."

Coral looked down at the gift then back up at me. Ginger shook it next to her ear like she thought it might make noise.

"What does it do?" Coral asked. "It's not poison, is it?"

Wow, these out-of-towners were harsh.

I laughed it off, trying to ignore the twisting sensation in my gut. Too soon to be making jokes about poison, wasn't it?

"No. Really. The Curious Cauldron is an apothecary and potion shop. I know coming to town and seeing a horrible incident like that isn't how you wanted to spend the week, so I wanted to make it up to you. It's something I use when I'm feeling stressed, and I thought it would help you too."

"This is a potion?" Ginger tilted the vial back and forth now, watching the liquid inside.

"Yes. It's all-natural, made with local ingredients. You put it on like perfume and it helps to calm the nerves."

She popped off the cork and took a cautious sniff. Her expression changed in an instant. "Oh, you're right. That does smell good."

I tried not to look *too* self-satisfied. I knew I had a good product, and helping people was what I did best.

Even Coral followed suit after Ginger's reaction. Thanks be, it managed to calm her foul mood a little.

All part of the plan.

A bell rang from behind us and out came Ronnie. He pushed a cart piled high with dishes. The smells of the feast hit me all at once, and immediately my mouth started watering.

Beef stew. Gravy. Thick, crusty bread. Fresh vegetables. Dinner at the Starlight didn't disappoint.

I even had a glass of wine with dinner — something I normally didn't do. Conversation flowed easily despite our differences. Food was the great equalizer, after all.

The first course meshed into the second, then a third. I thought I couldn't eat another bite and even Albus curled up beneath me in a satiated slumber, but then the desserts came out.

"Well," I joked to the nearby guests, "I guess I have a little more room for dessert."

A man with spiky black hair agreed. He sat a few seats down from m. I hadn't caught his name, but his voice boomed louder than the rest. Probably amplified by the wine. "I have an extra stomach just for dessert. That's the rule."

I snickered. Out came the chocolate cake, ice cream, pastries, and yes — even the pie I brought from home.

Finishing it off with a mug of steaming black coffee was the perfect capstone for the evening. By the time the plates were cleared away, I thought they might have to roll me to the door. I hadn't eaten so much good food in...well, ever.

The rest of the room looked similarly pleased. The disdain and skepticism of earlier washed away, helped along by the food and wine.

I may have overindulged a little — okay, maybe a lot — but I still had a job to do. I steered my muddled thoughts back to the task at hand and reviewed what I'd learned.

Coral had an attitude about her, while Ginger had a softer demeanor. She seemed to be the only one that did around here.

Even though we were all at the same dinner table, tension and rivalry still hung in the air, thick as molasses. It lessened as the night went on, but one thing was for sure: these contestants weren't exactly friends.

Not that I expected them to be — it *was* a competition, after all. The warm and cozy atmosphere of the Starlight mitigated most of it, but not all.

Man, I had no idea baking was so cutthroat. I gulped at the mental image. Hopefully not *literally* cutthroat.

With that grim thought on my mind, Ronnie entered the dining room one last time. No trays of food or drink preceded him this time. Simply him and big, charming smile. His face was flushed from running about the kitchen. His white hair stuck out a bit in places and his apron was smeared with grease, but his eyes told the real story.

This was what he loved.

"Now that we've filled our bellies, I wanted to give ye a warm welcome to our town." He rubbed his own stomach and beamed at the long table of guests. All eyes turned to face him.

"I do regret that ye had to visit our Haven in such...troubling times." He frowned and ran a nervous hand over his beard. "I can assure ye that Haven is a very safe place under normal circumstances. I don't want anyone gettin' the wrong idea."

I had to suppress a snicker. He wasn't lying, but lately...people were dropping like flies. Usually with me around.

I rolled my eyes. Maybe I really was cursed.

"I want ye to feel safe and welcome here," Ronnie continued, "so if there's anythin' I can do, let me know. The Starlight, and by extension meself, provide only the best hospitality Haven has to offer."

His eyes flickered over to mine. I gave him a subtle thumbs up.

"I don't know about you all," Coral started. She folded her napkin and placed it back on top of the table. "But I think I'm about to have a food coma. Thank you, though, for the warm words and pleasant company. The spread was delicious."

Ronnie bowed his head in thanks. "Yer always welcome at my table."

Before she turned for the stairs, Coral gave a

final glare at Ginger, then gestured to me. "Could I talk to you for a second?"

I perked up. "Me?"

"Yeah, won't take long. Come, follow me."

Sharing a glance with Albus, I got up and followed her into the hallway and toward the stairs. "What's the matter?"

"I'm sure you noticed who was missing at dinner." She didn't even turn to face me, just kept walking. I nearly had to jog to keep up.

"Yeah. Meryl. You think she's up to no good?"

"Oh, I *know* she's up to no good. Why do you think I came here in the first place?"

That stopped me in my tracks. "Wait, so you're not a baker?"

"I am," she continued, "but Meryl's been ruining the competition circuit for too long. Did you know she's been accused of cheating no less than six times?"

I raised an eyebrow. "Then why hasn't she been banned?"

Coral stopped at the third-floor landing and leaned against the wall, arms crossed. "That's the question, isn't it?"

That had my brain gears turning. Was Coral investigating too? Had I underestimated her? Albus poked his head out from behind my leg and approached her, sniffing her shoe. He immediately sneezed not once, but three times.

"Bless you!" Coral laughed. She bent down to pet him but he bolted back to me.

Interesting. Albus usually loved new people.

"Sorry about that," Coral said. "When I was prepping in my hotel room I knocked over a bottle of wine — boom, right on the shoes." She grimaced. "I got them dried out, but the stain and the smell I wasn't so lucky with. And seeing how I'm traveling... didn't bring any other shoes. Oops?"

Oof. That had to suck. "My friend Ruby's a tailor witch, she could probably help you out. I can put you in touch if you want."

Coral shook her head. "That won't be necessary. These old shoes I was about to throw out anyway." Her eyes drifted for a moment, then she snapped back to attention. "Do you think you could help me with something?" Her voice dropped. She took a step closer.

"Depends on what it is. I've got a shop to run and other responsibilities I need to take care of."

"Oh, it's nothing big." She waved her hands casually. "I've been trying to get Meryl to talk to me, or at least eavesdrop on her, but she's gotten smart. She suspects me, but she doesn't suspect you. Do you think you can get some information for me?"

At first blush, I wanted to say no. But I was planning to seek Meryl out next, and if I could gain favor with Coral (who was still a suspect) at the same time...

"What do you need?"

"I think she's in her room right now. Go talk to her, if you can. See what you can find out. I have my own theories, but like I said. I'm too far into this to see properly anymore. I need an outsider's point of view."

I took a deep breath. Okay. I could do this. Extending my hand, I shook with her — as I did so, a strange spark zapped between us. I gasped and yanked my hand away, shaking it. "Sorry," I hissed. "Static."

"See you later, Kat." Coral turned the corner, unlocked her door — number 307, I noted — and stepped inside.

"Wait —" I called out, but it was too late.

Albus looked up at me. "So now we have double reason to find Meryl. But the question is — what room is she staying in?"

CHAPTER ELEVEN

Luckily for me, I could figure that out pretty easily. I raced back down the stairs and over to the reception desk. A young woman, probably still a teenager, sat at the counter.

Ronnie must be busy in the kitchen or elsewhere. That wasn't unusual, but if I wanted to get Meryl's room number he was the person to talk to.

"Can I help you?" The girl asked as I approached the desk.

"Yes, I'm looking for Ronnie?"

"Just a moment please." She turned in her swivel chair. "Dad!"

I blinked and drew back a few inches. Her shout was not only sudden but ear-splittingly loud.

So this was Ronnie's daughter.

No answer came after a few moments. I didn't

think it was possible, but she shouted even louder. "Dad!"

A crash and a thump. A groan. "What?" The call came back nearly as loud.

"Someone here to see ya!"

I raised my eyebrows and looked down at Albus. He hunkered down on the floor, covering his ears with both paws.

After a few more mutters and sounds of movement, Ronnie emerged. The annoyance on his face all but disappeared when he recognized me.

"Ah, Kat." He glanced down at his daughter. Now that they were standing side by side, I could see the resemblance. "I see yeh met Helen."

I bowed my head. "Nice to meet you, Helen."

The bored expression on her face didn't leave. "Likewise." She drawled.

"Is everything all right?" Ronnie ran a hand over his beard.

"It's great. And dinner was scrumptious, as usual. I've got a question for you, though."

"Shoot."

I didn't waste a moment, spitting out the question before I could change my mind. "Is Meryl Mason staying here?"

"Hmm..." he thought for a moment. "Yes, I think so. She's one of them bakers?"

"Correct."

Ronnie's face changed as if he only just now realized what I was asking. "Why do ya want to know?"

Time to think fast. I held up the gift bag. "I was giving these to each of the guests as a welcome gift, and Meryl wasn't able to get hers since she wasn't at dinner. I wouldn't want her to miss out."

He extended his hand. "No problem. I can save it here behind the desk and hand it over next time I see her."

I opened my mouth, then closed it. *No, that wouldn't work at all.*

"I would really rather deliver it myself." I plastered on my best innocent smile and hoped for the best. "The Curious Cauldron is known for its personal touch — I want to embody that."

"Hmm," Ronnie said again. "I suppose yer right." He eyed the clock. "It's getting late. Yer not planning to visit now, are ya?"

I clenched my jaw. "Um, maybe?" I shrugged. "It will just be a quick visit, I promise. And if she's not in there or she doesn't answer the door, I promise I'll let you look after it." I held my breath and fluttered my eyelashes, hoping to change his mind. "Deal?"

Ronnie groaned after a few moments of deliberation. "Oh, all right. But make it snappy."

"I will, I promise." At this point, I was nodding my head like one of those bobble dolls, too caught up in the momentum to care. "Room number?"

"Let me see." He leaned over the counter and put on a pair of reading glasses. He tapped a few keys on the computer and squinted at the monitor. "Room 205. Second floor on the left."

With that, he straightened and gave me his most serious look yet. "Don't make me regret my decision, Kat. With everything that's been going on lately..." He shook himself. "I don't like it one bit."

"I'll be careful," I promised him. "You're a lifesaver, Ronnie. Don't forget that!"

"Eh, I'll try not to."

It took willpower not to take off at a sprint back down the hall. The adrenaline rush still had me on a high, practically vibrating with anticipation. I left the running to Albus and followed him back to the stairs.

At the second floor landing, I turned to Albus and took a deep breath.

"You ready for this?"

"I'm always ready...are *you*?"

"That's the million-dollar question, isn't it?" I steeled myself and opened the door, turning down the left passage as Ronnie instructed.

The rooms were odd-numbered on this side of the inn.

Two-oh-one, two-oh-three...

There it was. Room 205.

The hall was quiet this time of night. I tried to peer under the door to see any light within, but it was too tightly sealed.

Just moments ago I had been filled with energy and determination to find Meryl and uncover some of the secrets she'd been hiding. This was a perfect opportunity to get her alone, and yet...

My stomach twisted and growled. This was a potential killer we were talking about. If she really was the culprit, she could do to me whatever she'd done to Fabio...

"Tell me you have a plan," Albus said, noticing my tense demeanor.

I coughed out a nervous laugh. "Besides winging it? I didn't think I would get this far, honestly. Planned to talk to her during dinner."

"You can't wing everything, Kat." Albus scolded me. "If humans were meant to wing it, they would have wings."

"Haha." I knew Albus was trying to cheer me up but now wasn't the time.

"Want me to stay outside and guard the door while you chat?"

"Aww, are you my little guard kitty now?" The

thought of him patrolling the hall like some sort of scout was too amusing to ignore.

"You know what, I changed my mind." He shrunk away and shook himself. "I'm coming with you."

I rolled my eyes and gathered the last of my courage. "Well, here goes nothing." I raised my hand and knocked on the door three times. The noise rang out across the hallway, eerily loud at this time of night.

I glanced down at Albus. Would she answer? Was she even in her room? I was about to find out.

A few more seconds passed, lingering on toward a minute with no response. My shoulders slumped and I let out a sigh. "Guess she's not there. Or she doesn't want visitors."

"Oh well," Albus slunk back down the hall toward the stairs. "Was worth a try."

The moment I turned away, the door opened a crack.

"Hello? Is someone out there?"

I whirled around, heart in my throat. "Yes! Um, hi. Meryl?" I waved at her through the crack in the door. "It's me, Kat."

I couldn't see much in this lighting, but her hair stood up in a big rat's nest and makeup ran down her face.

"Oh," Meryl sniffed and wiped one eye. "It's you. I thought — well, never mind that."

Now this, I hadn't expected. Meryl was clearly distraught and crying about something. But what?

"If you can't tell I'm kind of a mess right now," Meryl continued. "Go away."

I should have taken her at her word, but I wasn't going to stand down that easily. In fact, this played right into the gift basket almost too well...

"I'm really sorry to bother you. Clearly, it's a bad time. I missed you at dinner and I had gifts for each of the guests. It's a potion to soothe the nerves if that helps right now."

"A potion?" The door opened a smidge wider, but the chain still held it in place.

"I'm an Earth witch," I explained. "Well, more specifically, a potion witch." I tilted my head downward. "This is my familiar, Albus."

"Meow."

"Can I come in?"

Meryl tensed. She looked over her shoulder. Wiped her eyes again. "This potion of yours, it will help?" Her voice wobbled, not at all like the brash, arrogant woman we'd met at the competition.

"It will," I promised. I held one hand up, fingers splayed, while placing the other across my chest.

"I'm not here to hurt you. I swear on the Witches' Code."

Any witch worth her salt knew that kind of vow was not made in vain. With that realization, Meryl's face softened. She unlatched the chain from the door and opened it completely. "Okay. Come in."

CHAPTER TWELVE

After seeing the room, I came up with a new nickname for the ill-fated competitor: Messy Meryl.

Perhaps it wasn't right for me to judge, especially since she was going through something, but I had to wade through dirty clothes and dodge discarded couch cushions just to get inside.

Albus, of course, loved every moment of it. He set to exploring all the nooks and crannies like this was his personal kitty obstacle course.

"Um, sorry for the mess." Meryl rushed around and cleared off a spot on the worn couch, beckoning me over. "I've just been so distraught since...you know. Since it happened."

I sat down next to her. Even Albus approached,

sniffing at her curiously before hopping up onto the couch for pets.

"Why don't you tell me about it." I kept my voice calm, even. Friendly. Opening the gift bag, I pulled out the small vial and handed it over. "I made this from scratch just this week. It's a combination of herbs and magic to ease the mind."

"Huh." She tilted the vial back and forth. "How does it work?"

"A witch can't give away all her secrets, can she?"

"How do I know this isn't poison?" She narrowed her eyes. "I still don't trust you, you know."

I expected that. In this situation, I wouldn't trust me either. But I'd gotten this far, and that had to count for something. "Here, I'll prove it to you." I reached back into the bag and pulled out a vial of my own, an extra I'd prepared just in case.

"I'll use it too. Same potion, same ingredients."

Meryl pursed her lips in thought. She looked from her vial to mine then back again. "I'll do it," she said with a mischievous smile, "if I can switch my vial with yours. Just so I know you don't have the safe one."

My eyes widened. I hadn't expected that. Clever. I didn't have anything to hide, though.

"Sure." I handed it over easily enough. "Both are the same, I promise. But I know you have no reason to trust me. Oh," I added. "And you don't drink it. You just sniff it — it's aromatherapy."

That seemed to convince her. Or at least quell some of her fears. We clinked our vials together and popped the corks. I showed her how to do it — I wafted it under my nose, then dabbed a bit on my wrists and neck.

"See?" I said, already feeling the cool, calming sensation flow through me. "No harm done."

"Huh," Meryl said again. She peered at the colored glass again. "That's actually not bad."

"How do you feel?" I asked.

"I feel..." She straightened her back. Stretched out her shoulders. Blinked. "Pretty good, actually. What's in that stuff?"

"It's my secret recipe. Been in the family for generations."

"Well, whatever it is, it's good. Can I keep this?" She dangled the vial.

"Of course. It's yours."

She slipped it into a bag by her side. "Potion witches. Huh. Wouldn't mind having one of them back home."

"It's a useful skill to have," I agreed. "Keeps me in business." I tapped my chin at a new thought. "Baking isn't so different from potions. Both involve gathering ingredients and putting them together in a certain pattern."

"You have a point." She glanced away, pressing her lips together, then, softly: "you're not as bad as I thought you'd be."

"Excuse me?" Albus yelped. Good thing Meryl couldn't understand him. My face flushed with the compliment — at least, I think it was a compliment? "Um...thanks?"

She still didn't meet my gaze. Even though we'd built a tiny bit of rapport and the potion helped calm both of our nerves, I could still tell something was wrong.

I turned the words over in my mind a few times, trying to phrase my question in a way that wouldn't put her back on her guard.

"I know everyone's been asking you about what happened at the tournament. That must be really stressful."

Meryl sniffed. "Yeah. It has been. I've been on the competitive circuit for a while but I've never seen anything like this..."

Digging a little deeper, I added, "I know you probably don't want to talk about it, but you're one of the top faces in the field. If anyone knows all the key players here, it's you."

That's right: appeal to her vanity.

She sat up a little straighter. Her lips turned upward, only slightly. "Oh. Thank you for saying so."

"It's true," I continued. This wasn't a time for moderation — time to lay it on thick. "You've won how many tournaments now?"

"Six." She didn't even have to think. "This was going to be my lucky number seven."

"Until one of the judges dropped dead."

Her shoulders shook as another sob threatened to spill over, but the calming tincture did its job. Her muscles relaxed. Her face softened. She said only one word. A soft, mournful whisper.

"Fabio."

"Did you know him?"

She let out a derisive snort. "Yeah. You could say that."

"What do you mean?" I tried to press as much as I could without being pushy or too personal, but I was *this close* to the line. If I said the wrong thing now, all bets were off.

"Well, I guess it doesn't matter now..." Meryl's voice trailed off. After a moment, she turned to face me full-on. Her eyes glimmered, still wet with tears, but full of conviction. "We were lovers."

I couldn't help sucking in a breath. That...I hadn't expected. "You and Fabio?"

She nodded, wincing. "Ever since the first time I

watched his cooking show, I knew I loved him. It didn't matter that he was married. Everything else was just a matter of fate. You have to understand..." She paused, shaking her head. "I never thought in all my wildest dreams that he would ever look at someone like me."

"And how did Fabio feel about this?" I kept my voice as calm, as neutral as possible.

On the inside, I had my bucket of popcorn, ready for the next installment of the juicy tale.

"He seemed to really care about me. We went on a few secret dates. Started seeing one another regularly just six months ago. With his influence and my talent, we swept the competition circuit."

By cheating? I wasn't crazy enough to say that, but that's what it sounded like. I glanced down at Albus, who returned with a knowing stare. This was good stuff — I didn't want to forget a single detail.

"Did anyone know?" I asked. *And more importantly, did Agent Hunt know about this?*

Meryl shook her head. "I thought at first he was ashamed to be with me, but it was more than that. Neither of us could continue competing or judging if we were found out, and even though we loved each other? We loved baking even more. We did what we had to do to keep our secret safe."

Another terrifying notion popped into my head,

though. A jilted lover might be so distraught that she would find a way to take it out on her lover — permanently.

Was I sitting next to a killer?

"I'm very sorry for your loss," I heard myself say. "I had no idea — no wonder you've been holed up in here crying." I reached over and grabbed an overturned box of tissues.

Jackpot! There was one left. I pulled it out and handed it over to Meryl, who blew her nose loudly.

"Thank you," she whispered. "I haven't had a chance to tell anyone. I was afraid if they knew, they would think I did it."

Well, actually...

"I want to help you, Meryl. I don't know what happened either, but I want to make sure we get justice for Fabio. He shouldn't have had to go like that. I know it won't bring him back, but if we can figure out what happened and why..."

"You want to know if I know anyone who had it out for him." Her tone of voice made it clear this was a statement of fact, not a question. "If I know anyone or anything that might have done it."

"Anything you can tell me would be helpful. You might have the clue we need to honor Fabio's memory."

She sniffed again and gave me a small, sad smile.

"I'll tell you one thing. I saw that Ginger girl snooping around the area with a camera before it all started. Don't know what she was up to, didn't ask, but now that I think of it, that was pretty odd."

"Ginger, the other baker in the competition?"

"Yes."

"If you saw that she was there early, then you must have been there too."

She drew back as if shocked. "*I* had an interview. I had a *reason* to be there."

"Can anyone confirm that?" *Man, I really did sound like one of those detectives on TV now.*

"Yeah, my agent." She picked up a soiled napkin and scribbled a phone number on it before handing it to me.

Okay, ew. I pinched it by a corner, trying not to gag. "Um, thank you." I set it aside. "Ginger could have arrived early to get a feel for the location. Maybe she worried about being late. What makes you think she's suspicious?"

"It's the quiet ones you have to look out for. Through this whole fiasco, who's been first to leave? Ginger. Who never speaks up? Ginger. Who makes herself scarce just at the right time?" She scowled. "I don't trust her."

"Well, Albus." I leaned back and stretched. "Looks like we have a new lead."

"Meow."

I got up and brushed myself off before extending my right hand. "Thank you for your time, Meryl. I really am truly sorry for your loss."

She hesitated for a split second but took my hand. "Thank you for listening," she said at last. "Sometimes it feels like no one else will." Meryl looked up and made eye contact. "And thank you for the potion. That was actually pretty incredible."

"So is kitchen witching," I pointed out. "In hindsight, I'm kind of glad I didn't get to be part of the competition. I would have burned the place down."

I laughed at myself and Meryl joined. It was good to see a smile on her face again. "I know we got off on the wrong foot, but I appreciate you talking to me." I turned for the door.

"Be careful out there," Meryl called after me. "And blessed be."

That warmed my heart. "Blessed be."

"What do you make of it?" Albus asked as soon as we were back outside. The moonlight shone down on us, lighting our way home along the deserted roads and sidewalks.

"Mixed feelings," I answered honestly. "On the one hand, she's a lot nicer than when I first met her. I can kind of understand why she was so crass before, and why she is so upset now. That doesn't mean it really gives her an excuse, but..."

"Do you think she killed Fabio?"

"There's the whole secret love affair thing...but she was so broken up and shocked about the murder. I don't think it was her."

"Unless she was frustrated that Fabio wouldn't make their relationship public."

"Is that something to kill over, though?"

Albus kept trotting along silently. "We've seen weirder. Or at least, I have."

I sighed. Unfortunately, he had a point. "We've got another lead to look into now, at least."

"I don't know about you, but I need a nap first."

I laughed, bent down, and petted him behind his ears. "I wasn't talking about right now! I'm tired too. We'll get back to work in the morning. Deal?"

"Deal," Albus said, as we drove the rest of the way home.

As I lay in bed that night, tossing and turning, one question kept repeating itself in my head: was Ginger's aloof, innocent demeanor all an act?

CHAPTER THIRTEEN

The doorbell startled me out of a weary sleep. I opened my eyes only a slit, trying to figure out if the sound was real or my dream. Sunlight peeked in through the blinds. A bird chirped right outside my window.

"I'll turn you into bird stew," I grumbled sleepily. The bird didn't care. It hopped over to the next branch, looked me right in the eye through the blinds, and chirped again. Loud.

I hadn't finished wincing from the sudden noise when the doorbell chimed again.

"Ughh." I rolled over and folded the pillow over my head. What *was* it with everything trying to wake me up today?

Maybe if I stayed here in bed and didn't turn on

any lights, the visitor would leave. Maybe. Was that too much to ask?

Ding-dong!

From my pillow cocoon, I felt Albus' weight jump onto the mattress. He dug his forepaws into my side, claws retracted, and pressed down.

"What..." I mumbled through the pillow. "Not you too."

"I thought you'd like to know who's at the door. I hopped up on the couch and peered out the window to check."

He didn't answer, and I so didn't feel like playing twenty questions. "Okay, who?"

"Emily!"

"What?!" Well, *that* woke me up. I sat upright so fast Albus flew off the bed and landed on all fours with a high-pitched squeak.

"Excuse you!" Albus scolded.

"Are you serious?" I asked breathlessly, my heart racing as I pulled on a robe and put my hair up in a ponytail to keep it out of my face.

"Yup. She waved at me and everything."

"Finally!"

I sidestepped him and rushed past. Fumbling with the lock, I threw open the front door. And there she was.

"Emily!" I gasped.

"Kat!" She threw herself into my arms and I hugged her with all my might, heart racing with both fear and excitement.

"Oh my gosh," I panted. "I was so worried about you! You didn't call, you didn't text, no one would tell me anything..."

Emily rolled her eyes. "Yeah, and it wasn't all roses for me either. Let's go in. You're going to want to hear this."

I didn't like the sound of that. A fraction of the joy melted away, a lingering dread in its place. Still, I ushered her into the house.

We plopped onto the worn couch like we had so many times before, but this time was different. Emily's face was white as a ghost — and believe me, I'd seen a ghost or two in my day — and her hands shook. She pawed at the worn afghan, fiddling with the loose threads and keeping her gaze down.

Albus followed but stayed at a distance. Something was wrong, that much was obvious, but what?

I scooted over a little closer and draped one arm over her shoulder. She didn't push me away, but she didn't react, either.

I chewed my lip for a few moments in thought. There was never going to be a 'right' thing to say, so I went with my gut. "Do you want to talk about it?" I asked softly.

"Yes," she said at length. "I do. I will. I mean..." Emily clamped her hands on either side of her head. "It's just...a lot."

"You can tell me." I rubbed her back in a small circle between her shoulder blades. The muscles there had locked into tense knots. "It's okay."

Even Albus jumped into action. He didn't say anything but gently rubbed up against Emily's legs before resting his head against her. His weight and warmth always grounded me in the worst of situations. I hoped it would do the same for her.

"Have you been home yet?" The thought came to me as I took in her tired, blanched face, and wrinkled clothing. The same clothing she'd worn the day of the competition.

Just what had they *done* to her?

"Stay right here. I'm going to get something, I'll be right back."

I got up and headed into the kitchen. Throwing open the cupboards, I prayed I still had doses of the soothing serum pre-made. I'd given most of them out during the event at the Starlight, but I usually kept one or two around, just in case of emergency...

"Ah!" I had to reach way back in the corner

where only dust bunnies lived, but I found an old, forgotten vial. Perfect.

Next, I took a mug and filled it with steamed milk and honey before tipping the contents of the vial into the mixture. It flashed a pale sky blue before dissolving. Yes, I knew it was more of an aromatherapy potion, but with the extra milk and honey to dilute it, it would have the same effect.

When I returned to the living room, Albus was still keeping Emily company. She'd unclenched her shoulders at least a little bit and sat more expansively. One leg propped up on the coffee table while the other curled under her. Her head lolled to the side, resting against the plush cushions.

"Here. Drink this." I sat down the mug on the side table and crouched down to be at eye level. "I made it just for you."

"One of your potions?" Emily said. Her voice was still distant.

"One of my potions," I confirmed. "It will help your nerves. Drink it."

She didn't protest, thank goodness for small miracles. Emily brought the mug to her lips and drank. Almost immediately, the magic began its work. I could practically see the calm passing through her body with each sip. Neither of us spoke until she finished, and when she set the mug back down on the saucer and looked up at me, her face was much more composed.

"Thanks," Emily said. "I really needed that."

"What is family for?" I circled around to sit next to her on the couch again. I took her hands in mine. "Now tell me, Em. What happened? Are you okay?"

Her lips tilted upward in a sad smile. "That's a loaded question if I've ever heard one. I'll start at the beginning, I suppose..."

"They asked me the same things over and over. What I knew, what I did. Trying to get a confession out of me, I suppose. Don't know why they were so convinced in the first place."

"That's ridiculous. It could have been an accident, for all we know. Maybe Fabio was having some health problems beforehand."

"I told them that. They didn't want to hear it." She shrugged. "Told me they found magical residue on the pan used to serve the pie. Not only that — dark magic."

I sucked in a breath. "What — how —"

"According to them, it was cursed. And since I was the one that served them on that pan, well..."

"You didn't do anything, though!" I clenched my

fists, temper already rising. "That 'agent' better hope he doesn't run into me again. I wanna give him a piece of my mind." Taking a deep breath, I composed myself. I wasn't even the traumatized one in this situation. I needed to be present — to be strong for Emily.

"I know I didn't. They're the ones that had a problem with that." She threw her hands up in the air. "I don't even know any curses!"

"Not many people do."

"Hence why the PEA showed up," Emily pointed out. "Only they've got the wrong witch."

"Well, you're here now, so they must have had a reason to let you go." My mouth dropped open. "Or you escaped?"

Emily laughed. "No, nothing so dramatic as that."

"So what changed?"

"I got tired of being there. I got tired of doing the same song and dance. They were getting tired of it too, I could tell. So I finally came up with an ultimatum. 'Bring your most powerful truth serum,' I said, 'and you'll get your answers once and for all.'"

I put a hand to my mouth. "Do you have any idea how rare Truth Serums are? I'm not just talking about those teas I make. They help lower inhibitions and increase trust, but they don't physically force the truth out of a person. The Serum, on the other hand..." I shuddered. "There's a reason it's so highly regulated that almost no one can get their hands on it."

Emily nodded. "I knew that. Which is why it was the perfect play to show them I was serious. You should have seen their faces when I suggested it." She smiled at the thought. "They didn't know what to do with themselves."

"I would think not." My mind still raced. I gaped at Emily's courage and quick thinking. "Don't tell me they actually gave you Serum."

"They had a good long talk about it. Scared them a little bit, I think. But they called my bluff. Who knows where or how they got it, but within a matter of hours they came back with that horrible golden vial."

My eyes widened. My pulse quickened. "They didn't."

"They did," Emily promised. "And let me tell you. Yuck. That stuff was gross!"

"I can't believe you went through with it." My hand still covered my mouth in shock. "I've never seen any in real life before."

"I couldn't exactly back down after I was the one that suggested it, could I?" She dug her fingers deeper into the loose strands of the afghan, clenching them close to her body. "But I wasn't afraid. I didn't have anything to hide. At least, not about the whole curse conundrum."

"Bet you gave them quite the shock when they realized you actually were telling the truth."

"Oh yeah." Emily's eyes widened as she nodded. "They were mad. But what could they really do? I answered every question, even under Serum. They couldn't keep me any longer. I got my butt out of there before they changed their minds. Ended up here. I haven't even been home yet."

"Wow." That was all I had left in me. I held out my arms and drew her into a warm, tight hug. "I'm so glad you're all right. You must have walked for ages..."

"And my feet are still fussing at me about that." Emily tugged off her shoes and wiggled her toes. "Aaah."

"You must be famished." I realized. I stood up and looked toward the kitchen, then back to her. "I'm willing to bet they didn't feed you much, if at all."

"A little, yeah, but what I wouldn't give for some real food..."

"I know you're the kitchen witch, but let me make you something. Just this once."

"Even if I wanted to," Emily stretched her legs

and closed her eyes, laying back against the cushions, "I wouldn't have the energy to stop you."

After we'd gotten some food in our bellies, we both felt a little better. The potion, the warm blanket, and the comfort of home all helped to soothe our nerves. I didn't press Emily for any more information. She had been through a lot in such a short time. Poor girl looked exhausted.

"Um," Emily spoke up, her gaze still downcast. "Do you mind if I stay here for a bit?" She clenched and unclenched her fists. "I don't really want to be alone right now, and if I went to my mom's, well... she'd end up asking too many questions."

I gave her a sympathetic smile. "I totally get that. My mom is the same way. Cut from the same cloth, those two."

"They *are* sisters, after all."

"But to answer your question, yes. You can stay here as long as you need. You know you're always welcome here. You're family."

We hugged once more, and this time, my eyes were the wet ones. If only I had known...I frowned at that line of thinking.

There was nothing I could have done, I knew

that, but imagining Emily all alone with those terrible people, not knowing if she'd ever escape or see the light of day again...

That wasn't the PEA I knew.

And just like that, another mystery piled itself onto my plate. First Fabio's mysterious murder, then the cursed cuisine, the cunning competitors, and this illicit investigation. Things were heating up here in Haven, and not in a good way.

CHAPTER FOURTEEN

Thankfully, the Curious Cauldron was closed today. I had too much on my plate to worry about going into the store right now. Even if I did, I wouldn't be able to keep my mind from jumping all over the place.

Generally, I was pretty good at compartmentalizing, but the recent events one after another had fried that ability to a crisp. Now I felt like a swimmer adrift at sea, unable to reach an anchor point, at the mercy of the waves.

So it was well enough to spend the day with my cousin. Especially after what she'd gone through at the hands of the supposed Paranormal Enforcement Agency. The more I thought about her story, the more disgusted and horrified I felt. Their tactics in this case were nothing less than draconian. There was a lot at stake here, sure, and I knew they had to take it seriously, but they'd essentially kidnapped Emily on mere suspicion. It wasn't until she opted into a very dangerous truth serum that they let her go at all. If she hadn't...would she still be there?

I shuddered. If this was how they really were, ex-Mayor Armstrong's paranoia made a little more sense. Not that it excused what he did, but...

After Emily showered, she came out into the living room wearing only a towel. "So here's the thing. Those clothes I came in wearing smell like death and have days worth of grime on them. I'd ask if you had anything I could wear, but, well..." She looked me up and down. "I'm a bit bigger than you."

A bit. Emily's love for baking showed in her figure — she sported plump curves where I'd always had a more slender frame. I searched my brain trying to think if I had anything that would fit her.

"What about that awful shirt you got from the Wilders?" Albus piped up, rounding the corner. He was still licking his chops from eating, only half listening to our conversation. "You know the one, Kat."

I snorted. Oh yes. There was no way he would ever let me forget that. As a prank, Kelly Wilder lent me a shirt when mine got destroyed. The only problem? It was the flashiest thing I'd ever seen and had a huge sequined message across the bust — "HEXY AND I KNOW IT."

Yeah, Albus had given me an earful about that one. Not to mention Chance and his brothers...

The shirt had been far too large for me, after all. I grinned and rubbed my hands together. "You know what, Emily? I've got just the thing."

"Where on *Earth* did you get this thing? I'd rather wear my old dirty clothes than this!" Emily held the shirt out in front of her at arm's length. If she could have held it away from her even further, she would have. The way she was looking at it, it might as well have threatened to bite or something.

"Beggars can't be choosers, Em." I cackled. "Come on, try it!"

"You've got to be kidding me," Emily grumbled. But to my surprise, she went along with it. She pulled the purple t-shirt over her head, scowling the whole time.

I had to hold my breath to keep from laughing — okay, it *did* look ridiculous. But if I had to suffer wearing that thing, then someone else would too. That's what friends are for, right?

"I'm gonna get you for this," Emily groused, still

staring at the abomination she now wore. "I am *so* gonna get you for this."

"I know, I know." I couldn't hold it in anymore. I snorted out a laugh, my shoulders shaking. "It's worth it though!"

"The curse of the hexy shirt continues," Albus drawled from the corner. "I wonder who the next victim will be?"

Sometimes, I was *really* glad not everyone could hear my cat talk.

"So what do you want to do today?" I asked Emily. "I have an errand to run, but I'm pretty much free. You can take a nap in my room if you want, while I go drop something off at Ruby's."

Emily shook her head. "I don't like the idea of staying cooped up here. Had enough of that." She looked up at me. "What's at Ruby's?"

"I borrowed a sewing kit from her the other day when I ripped a hole in my jeans." I pulled up my pant leg to show her the patched knee. "It's not glamorous, but it does the job."

"Good thing we have tailor witches, right?"

"Good thing," I agreed, "or I'd be in a lot of trouble." Just then an idea struck me. "Now that I think of it, I've got a coupon for Sew it Seams. You know, Ruby's boutique? She gave it to me after I did a favor for her son, but I never ended up using it."

"That's not for the all-inclusive personal styling session, is it? I couldn't take that from you." Even as she said so, though, her eyes lit up with envy.

"It is, and I'm not taking no for an answer. Let's go to Sew it Seams and get you something a little less...hexy." I couldn't hold back the wicked grin plastered across my face. I felt like the Cheshire Cat, and I was loving every moment of it.

Emily's mouth dropped open. "You mean I have to go *out* in this?"

I raised my eyebrows. "Do you want that personal styling session or not?"

"Oh, you are *definitely* getting it, Kat." She grumbled and pouted her way to the door. "Just you wait."

"After you, o hexy one!" I dipped into an elaborate bow. Emily walked past, but not without smacking me on the back of the head.

I deserved that.

We bickered and bantered our way back to the car. The mood had noticeably lightened, thank goodness for that, but the undercurrent of tension remained. Getting a good old-fashioned makeover was just what the doctor ordered.

The ride to Ruby's store Sew it Seams was pretty quiet. Even Albus didn't have much to say. He curled up in the back seat and closed his eyes. His tail wrapped around his body in a circle and he tucked his legs inward in a pose I liked to call a

"kitty cinnamon roll."

A few minutes before we arrived, Emily spoke up again. "I've been thinking about the case."

Uh oh. My hands tightened on the steering wheel. "And?"

"Once we get done at Ruby's, I have a proposition for you. The more I think about what happened, the more things don't add up. I need to check something back at the scene, but I'm not going alone. You up for a little midnight outing?"

How did I always get roped into these? "What are you looking for?" I kept my eyes straight ahead on the road, though my heart and my brain had other ideas. Back into the belly of the beast was the last place I wanted to be, and yet if we could find answers, find the truth...

"I can't say for sure." Emily twirled a ringlet of hair around her finger in thought. "I just know we need to go back. The agent said there was a curse, remember? I need to know if the curse was on everything, or specific to my station."

I pressed on the brake pedal a little too hard pulling up to a stop sign. We lurched forward in our seats, yanked by the restraints. "Sorry," I hissed. Albus made some very displeased sounds from the back seat and Emily rubbed her neck. "Sorry, you just caught me off guard. You don't mean to say someone cursed you specifically."

"I don't know." Emily frowned. "But I want to find out."

I made the final turn onto the main street where Sew it Seams shared a building with two other businesses. I pulled into a parking space, turned off the engine, and turned to Emily.

"We will," I promised her. "But first, we both need a little retail therapy."

CHAPTER FIFTEEN

Ruby looked up the moment the bell jingled over the door, announcing our arrival. Her eyes widened and she rushed over, drawing both of us into big motherly hugs.

"Oh my goddess, Kat. It's so good to see you. And you, Emily! I was so worried. Are you all right?"

Emily glared at me. I shrugged.

"What? Word spreads fast here in Haven."

Rolling her eyes, Emily sighed. "Now that the whole town knows my business..."

"Oh, don't worry," Ruby said. "You get used to it." She flitted across the store and stopped in front of a rack of clothes. "My family has been in the spotlight more often than not, of late. It was hard, having everyone coming in, asking questions.

Making assumptions. Still is hard. First with my husband passing away, and then my sweet Will..." She stopped, voice choking. It only lasted a moment. She regained her composure, but not so fast that I didn't notice her despair.

"I talked to him on the phone the other day," she continued. "Will, I mean. He's doing okay. Well, as okay as he can be in jail. He's keeping busy. Reading a lot of books, he said. He still wants to apply to college when he gets out. Make a better life for himself."

I nodded and put a hand on her shoulder. She'd gone through more than any woman should have to in such a short period. After her husband suddenly passed away, she was left with a struggling family business and a mountain of debt. Oh, and Will's mouth to feed.

The struggle continued until a newcomer moved into the shop next to Ruby's, trying to buy the lot out from under her. Tensions flared, tempers boiled, and Will ended up smack dab in the middle of it.

One poor choice led to another in a misguided attempt to protect his remaining family, leaving their rival dead and Will in a panic.

I was there when we talked him off the ledge. When we talked him into turning himself in, and promised him that there was life after this.

I prayed that was still true.

"He was a good kid," I reminded Ruby. "*Is* a good kid. He'll be out soon enough. Sheriff Cooper's working to get him out early, remember?"

Ruby sniffed. "Yeah. I remember." She shook herself. "But that's not why you came here today. I'm sorry. Can I help you with anything?"

"First of all," I said, pulling the sewing kit out of my bag, "thank you for letting me borrow the sewing kit. Second of all," I pulled out the embossed gift certificate next, "I'm ready to cash this in."

That instantly brightened her spirits. Nothing excited Ruby more than fashion. That, and I knew it gave her a good outlet for her grief. She clapped her hands together and yanked the certificate from my hand. "Oh, I'm so excited you finally decided to try it! We're going to make you look fabulous."

"It's not for me." I stepped aside and gestured at Emily. "It's for Em."

"Oh?" Ruby's voice rose in surprise. "Are you sure?"

I nodded. "I'm sure. She needs it more than I do."

For the first time, Ruby's eyes roamed over Emily's outfit, taking in the full horror of the hexy abomination. Maybe I was imagining things, but I could have sworn her face turned a little green.

"I...I see that. Oh my."

I put a hand over my mouth to hide my snicker. The reactions never got old.

"Well, right this way my dear. We'll get you fixed up in no time." She ushered Emily toward the back of the store while gesturing to me. "Do make yourself comfortable, Kat. We won't be but a moment!"

Yeah, I'd heard that one before.

I browsed the racks for a few moments before sitting down in one of the chairs in the front waiting area. Albus slurped water from a pet bowl near the door. I was just getting comfortable when the door jingled once more. I looked up and the man I saw there sent my world screeching to a halt.

Sheriff Hal Cooper.

"Well, if it isn't Kat Sullivan." He sauntered up to my chair and took off his hat. "Didn't expect to see you here today."

"Sh-sheriff," I stammered. My face flushed with heat. "I could say the same about you."

"I come here for my work shirts. Miss Ruby does the best work in town." He put his hands on his hips and looked around. "Say, where is she, anyway?"

"She's in the back with a customer," I pointed

out. "I'm sure she'll be back at any moment, though, if you can wait."

"I don't see why not." He plopped down on the chair next to mine, his cuffs jangling against his belt. He angled his body toward mine. "I haven't seen you around lately, Kat. What have you been up to?" With a grin, he added. "Surprised you haven't turned up any trouble again. Never thought I'd say this, but work's a bit boring after those murder cases."

I gulped. Before I could stop myself a nervous laugh bubbled up. *Yeah, about that...*

Cooper narrowed his eyes and tilted his head in question. "There's nothing you need to tell me, is there?"

"What?" I shook my head. "No." I knew full well lying to an officer was a bad idea, but what could I do? This case was strictly magical in nature, and the PEA — the "magic police", as it were — were already on top of it. Cooper couldn't get involved. The less he knew, the better.

"You just seem a bit jumpy, is all."

"I've been busy," I managed. "Even Ruby hasn't seen me in weeks. That's why I came over to say hi."

"Is that so?" He rubbed his chin. "I hope you're not working *too* hard. We're gonna have dinner one of these days, right?"

I bit my lip. *Oh, right. That.* "Of course. I haven't

had time lately, but I'll let you know when I'm free. I want to, I just can't commit to a time right now. You know how business can be." At least, I hoped he did.

"No, it's all right. I get it." He put his hands on his knees and looked down to see Albus standing there, sniffing his shoe. "This cat follows you everywhere, huh?"

"His name is Albus." I bent down and rubbed a hand over his shiny fur. "He's curious as they come and a real pain sometimes, but he's *my* pain."

"Spoken like a true animal lover." Cooper bent down and petted Albus between the ears. This time, Albus didn't shrink away. He leaned into the touch, knocking his head against Cooper's hand. "I used to have a cat of my own."

"Used to?"

"Dorothy. My sweet girl lived a good life."

"Oh." The feeling hit me at once. Losing a pet was never easy. I didn't know what I'd do if I ever lost Albus. "I'm sorry," I said softly, folding my hands in my lap.

"Yep." He cleared his throat. "But that's all in the past now." Cooper paused for a moment, then, "say, since you're here, I thought maybe you could help me with something. While we're waiting for Miss Ruby to finish up there in the back."

I raised an eyebrow. "Help with what?" The last

time he'd asked for my expertise there was an active murder investigation. Well, there was this time too, but he didn't know about it.

And it needed to stay that way.

"Have you heard from that boyfriend of yours?" He scowled the words as if they tasted foul.

"Huh?" That caught me off guard. Since when was the sheriff interested in my personal life? "Chance?" That was the only person he could mean. "He's not my boyfriend. We've spent some time together, but nothing serious." Whether I wanted it to be serious was another matter entirely.

"And you haven't heard from him?"

"No, why?" I crossed my arms.

Cooper didn't give me a chance to breathe. "Because I've been trying to get in touch with him but no response. Even drove by that garage him and his brothers work at. No cars. No nothing. Thought maybe you'd know where they'd gone."

I blinked and sucked in a breath. Albus tensed next to me, sensing danger. The Wilders were gone? I knew that Chance was worried about the PEA the last time I talked to him, but I didn't know they'd up and left.

"No," I said honestly. "I didn't know they left town."

"Odd," Cooper said after a moment. "But thank

you, that's all I wanted to know for now. I suppose they'll come back eventually."

"They always do," I pointed out. Hopefully, this time, I was right.

The curtain rings clicked together and ended the conversation. Emily and Ruby stepped out from the back room, and I could barely believe my eyes. Emily wore a shiny gold party dress — strapless with a fluffy bottom of tulle and lace. My mouth dropped open. Ruby had put Em's hair up in ringlets to fall gracefully around her face and her makeup further accentuated the glow that seemed to be pouring off of her.

Sheer leggings captured the curves of her hips and legs, ending in black flats. "One more thing," Ruby said, handing Emily a final garment. She shrugged on a black leather jacket to complete the look then did a little spin. The grin on her face was larger than I'd ever seen.

"How do I look?" Emily froze mid-spin when she saw Sheriff Cooper sitting there next to me. The wide-eyed grin dropped in an instant. "Wait a second — why is he here?"

"Not to worry, ma'am. I'm off duty." Cooper stood

and bowed his head in recognition. "I just came by to pick up some work shirts from Miss Ruby here."

"And I have them ready for you. Just come up to the counter here and I'll ring you up."

While Ruby processed Cooper's order, Emily joined me. "Is everything okay?" She hissed. "I feared for a moment word got out about..." she waved her hands. "You know."

"Be cool," I warned her in the same low tone. "He doesn't know anything, don't spoil it."

"Okay." Emily breathed a sigh of relief. "Sorry, just had me worried for a moment there."

"And you look stunning," I added, trying to change the subject. "I knew Ruby was good, but wow. Now you're making me wish I had used it on myself!"

Emily giggled. "I feel like a whole new girl, it's amazing!"

I patted her on the back and drew her into a hug. "You deserve it, after all we've been through lately. You look fab, and the best part?"

"What's that?"

"It's on the house! Seriously, can you imagine how much something like that must cost?"

She cringed. "I'd never be able to afford anything this fancy."

"And now you don't have to!"

Cooper sidestepped us on his way to the door, a bag in hand. He replaced his hat, tipping it to us. "Ladies."

I gave him a half-hearted wave and there he went, jingling his way back out the door.

Emily and I headed back to the counter where Ruby waited.

"This is really amazing, Ruby." Emily still stared in awe at her new outfit. "Thank you so much."

Ruby practically glowed. She bounced on the balls of her feet, smile as big as the sun. "It was my pleasure, darling. I know that dress isn't exactly the most casual getup, so I'm going to prepare two more outfits for everyday wear. The new fabric won't be in till next week, though, so you'll have to come back."

Both our mouths dropped open. "Seriously?" Emily crowed. "I thought there was only one outfit included in the deal!"

Ruby beamed. "I aim to overdeliver."

"Thank you again," Emily said, shaking Ruby's hand. "This means more than you know."

"All in a day's work." She waved as we turned to the door. "Don't be a stranger, now!"

We stood in the parking lot for a few moments before getting into the car. "So," I started, "now that you look totally fabulous, what do you want to do now?"

Emily gave me a small smile, though not as brilliant as the ones back in the store. "This is wonderful and all, but I can't help but think about what we talked about. You know, before coming here."

My heart sank. "Oh."

"There's something I want to do. But first, we're going to need to go see my dad."

CHAPTER SIXTEEN

"Your mom's gonna freak, isn't she?"

"Probably. Not as much as yours, though."

"Ain't that the truth." I laughed, thinking of my own mother. "I'd probably be put on house arrest for the rest of my life."

Emily snorted. "Don't think I'm looking forward to all the questions. But there's something there in my dad's shop that we are going to need for tonight."

"Wait...we're doing this tonight?" I pulled up to a stop sign and glared at her.

"Yeah, well...the sooner the better. If my theory is true, we need to get back to the scene. Fast."

I took a deep breath and sighed. "All right. I trust you. But I swear if I get kidnapped like you did..."

"You won't," Emily promised. "Trust me."

I tapped my fingers on the steering wheel nervously. "If you say so." As we pulled into the parking lot, I peered out the window at the darkening sky. "If those clouds open up, we are not going anywhere. Come on, let's get inside."

Emily stepped into the shop first, followed by Albus and me. Her dad — my uncle — owned an antique store constantly overflowing with knick-knacks. The real treasures, though, were upstairs in their private residence where Uncle Ben tinkered away on all manner of magical gadgetry.

"Emily!" Her mother, my Aunt Veronica, shrieked like a banshee and came running. Good thing I stepped out of the way just in time — she nearly bowled both Albus and me over in her excitement. I lost my balance and stumbled into a table stacked high with precious china.

The high-pitched jingle of plates and mugs stopped my heart for a split second. Luckily my instincts reacted faster than my brain did. I righted the table and the trinkets just in time.

Aunt Veronica crushed Emily in a bone-crunching hug, peppering her face with kisses. "Oh my goodness, child, I was so worried about you! Don't ever scare me like that again!"

"Ew, gross." Albus sidestepped the lot of us and slunk off through the labyrinth of boxes and shelves.

"Mom," Emily protested and pulled away. She scrubbed her face with the edge of her sleeve. "I'm fine, I promise. Well," she paused and gave a small shrug. "Mostly fine, but I need to see dad for a moment. Is he here?"

"No, hun, he went out for a moment. Don't think you're getting out of talking to me that easily." She put her hands on her hips. "I *will* be having a word with the so-called PEA about this. I don't care if I have to go all the way to HQ to do it."

"Mom..." Emily protested again. "If you'd just listen for one second. I have a plan."

Aunt Veronica tapped her foot. "Don't tell me you're going to go back out there. After what those... people...did to you?" She scowled as if calling them people was far too generous.

"Please." Emily's voice was pleading now, her eyes rimmed with tears. She took her mother's hands and leaned into her embrace once more. Mother and daughter, leaning on one another. Taking one another's strength.

"I promise I'll be okay. I know how to clear my name, but I've got to go back to the scene to do it."

"And I suppose you're going along with Kat, are you? She up to her old sleuthing tricks again?" My aunt clicked her tongue. "I swear, this family..."

"Her 'sleuthing tricks' have helped the last two

times, haven't they? It was because of us that we found out who killed Ian in the first place."

With a sigh, Aunt Veronica put a hand to her forehead and leaned against the counter, a rare spot of bare wood in the overstuffed shop. "You've always been headstrong, child. You and Sarah's girl, both. I don't suppose I'll be able to talk you out of this."

It was time for me to step in. "We wouldn't be doing this unless it was absolutely necessary."

She gave us a sad smile. "I know. I just worry about y'all, as a mother. Allow me that?"

"I love you, mom." Emily hugged Veronica and looked up into her eyes. "I will be back. I promise."

"You better." Aunt Veronica waggled her finger at us, but her tone had lightened. "And by the way, what on Earth are you wearing?"

"It's a long story...let's just say Ruby had a little gift for me."

Aunt Veronica beamed. "Well, it looks lovely."

Emily stepped around her mom and opened a cabinet in the large desk at the far corner of the room. "Mom, do you have the key to the attic?"

Aunt Veronica reached into her pocket and pulled out a keyring. She picked through each one and held up a vintage, wrought iron skeleton key. "Why do you need to get into the attic? It's just your dad's dumping ground for all his weird collections. I told him he better start consolidating up there — the floor's ripe to rot and I don't want anything crashing down on my head from the ceiling, thank you very much."

"One of those 'old, crusty gadgets,' as you call them, might have the powers we need to solve the case. I want to scan the area, see if there are any traces of wild magic, any curse residue. Weren't you the one that told me strong magic always leaves signs?"

Aunt Veronica nodded. "To those who know how to look for it, yes."

"And I do," Emily added, "but I'm just as concerned as you are. Believe me, I don't want to go back to the scene. I'd give anything not to have to. So that's why I'm thinking of a compromise — Kat and I can keep our distance and watch from cover. If we have something that can scan the area instead..."

"Clever idea." Aunt Veronica looked impressed. "Well, go on. See what you can find." She waved us toward the door leading up to the residence. "Just don't break anything up there, all right? Ben'll have both our heads!"

With that amusing mental image in mind, we unlocked the door and headed up to the living area. Crawling around in a dusty attic wasn't exactly suited for a fancy new dress, so she changed into something a little more comfortable first. Then we climbed the rickety old ladder, used the key, and pushed open the dusty, creaking trapdoor leading to the attic.

As I stared up into the storage area, a chill prickled at the back of my neck. *Magic.*

Emily clambered up into the room first and disappeared into the darkness. A few rustles and thuds of movement, then a tired squealing of long-forgotten metal.

Sunlight poured through a grimy skylight, throwing long shadows on the mountains of stuff within.

"Man, you weren't kidding about Uncle Ben being a hoarder."

I picked through the piles and boxes as best I could, but the sheer amount of mess up here made the antique store downstairs look like the height of organization.

"Why do you think my mom's been getting on his case for years?" Emily looked up from behind a cardboard box nearly as tall as she was. "He says he has a use for everything, and while I admire the resourcefulness, so much of this is just...junk." She pulled out an electric hand mixer — well, what used to be one. For some reason, the mixing blades had been replaced with pencils.

Emily rolled her eyes and tossed it aside, digging deeper.

"You made it sound like the attic was full of magical artifacts."

"Oh, it is." Emily looked up again, pulling cobwebs from her hair. "They're just mixed in with all the other junk."

"It would help if I knew what I was looking for." I flipped through a box of old magazines, wrinkling my nose at the musty smell.

"You'll know it when you see it," Emily promised me. "Or rather, when you feel it. When we opened the door, you felt all that magical energy coming out of here, right?"

"Yeah," I said. "Thought it was just me."

"Like I said," Emily repeated. "Magical artifacts. Follow the pulse of the energy, if you can. It's gotta be here somewhere."

I closed my eyes, took in a deep breath, and let it out. *Focus*, I repeated silently. *Focus*. Like sharpening the image on a microscope, the flow and ebb of magic slowly presented itself.

It floated and swirled through the air like so many particles of dust, and that's when I realized — the attic wasn't just filled with dust. Motes of magic held sway here as well.

I followed the "pulse", as Emily had called it, as

best I could. Unfortunately, my main skills lay elsewhere and I kept losing the trail. Finally, I found a big cloud of glowing energy surrounding a bookcase, pressed all the way up against the far wall. I had to watch my step — the floorboards creaked and groaned with each footfall, just like Aunt Veronica warned.

I didn't want to think about falling through the floor right now. Holding my breath, I kept my steps light.

"Find something?" Emily called out.

"Yeah...come here." I drew closer and reached out a hand to brace on the wall. The glow was coming from the bookshelf, all right, but the shelves were empty...

Or so it seemed.

Still holding onto the wall, I crouched down and looked at the bottom shelf where the highest concentration of energy rested. Brushing off the fine layer of dust, my fingers trailed across a strange crease with a divot I hadn't noticed before.

"Hey, check this out."

Emily stood behind me, putting a hand on my shoulder for support. "No way," she breathed.

I hooked my fingernail into the crease and pulled upward. A thin wood panel came free and exposed a hollow area beneath. "A secret compartment." I marveled and turned to look up at Emily. "You seeing this?"

"I am." She shoved a few boxes out of the way and joined me at my side, crouching to look into the small hidden drawer. "I've never actually seen one in real life before. Dad talks about them all the time, but I never knew how they worked..."

Putting the wood panel to the side, I squinted into the dim space. After pulling out my phone and using the flashlight app to get a better look, we both gasped in unison.

At first glance, it looked like a small remote control car. It was flat and long, with reflective panels on top. Four tough, treaded wheels would allow it to traverse difficult terrain. What was it for, though?

The magic positively spewed off of this thing, and yet I didn't know yet how a toy car could help us seek out any traces of magic at the crime scene.

"There it is!" Emily reached past me. Carefully she lifted it out of the compartment.

"What is it?" I had to ask. "You know I'm not good with gadgets."

"This," Emily said with satisfaction, "is what's going to save our bacon."

CHAPTER SEVENTEEN

"So what does this thing do?"

We moved away from the mess and found a rare empty spot on the floor. Emily sat cross-legged with the car in her lap while I sat alongside her.

"See these panels?" Emily pointed. "They collect and analyze magic in the air. Think of it as a solar panel."

"Huh, that's really neat. I had no idea that was even possible."

"Well if you'd stick your head outside of your greenhouse now and then, you'd see that magical technology has really advanced in the last few years." Her good-natured teasing stung, but she had a point.

I had my specialty, and I stuck to it. Unfortunately, that often meant being out of touch with other parts of the magical community. Thank goodness I had friends and family that balanced my strengths and weaknesses.

"So it's like a metal detector, but on wheels, for magic." I tried to put together a few familiar concepts together, hoping I was on the right track.

Emily laughed. "Pretty much exactly like that. So we can direct this thing to explore the scene and we don't even have to stick our necks out, as it were."

"What are we looking for?"

"Remember how I told you the utensils at my specific station appeared to be cursed?"

"Yeah..."

"What I want to find out is how far that dark magic spread. Was it just my station? Was it targeted? Or was I just at the wrong place at the wrong time? If we can prove that the curse couldn't have come from me, they'll have to look at other options."

I rubbed my chin, brain gears churning. "That's not a bad idea." I tried to stand and hit my head on a low hanging lamp. That in turn toppled me to the side where I had to grab onto a pile of musty cardboard boxes to keep from going down completely. I coughed away the dust. "We got what we came for. Can we go back downstairs and talk about it?"

"Fair enough." Emily waved her hand in front of her face. She sneezed, kicking up even more dust. "You know, the more time I spend up here the more I agree with my mom. This place is a mess."

I rolled my eyes. "That's an understatement." And I had thought Pepper was messy...

"Okay, let's go."

We headed down back into the living area and were about to go downstairs to the storefront once more, but voices carried up from the floor below.

Gruff, demanding voices.

"Wait," Emily hissed, holding up a hand to stop me. "That voice sounds familiar." She cracked open the door only barely.

We couldn't see much through the small gap. Not enough to see who was down in the shop, anyway.

The voice grew clearer. Grew closer.

"Are you telling me how to do my job, ma'am?"

Aunt Veronica spoke up. "Why yes, sir, I suppose I am. Now you either come back here with a notarized warrant or get the heck off my property."

Emily froze with fear next to me. My heart sank.

"It's him," Emily hissed. "Kat, it's him. He's here." Her face creased with fear. She looked to me for answers, wide-eyed.

"Let's see what happens," I hissed back. "Your

mom has some fire in her, going up against them like that."

"Shh—" Emily interrupted. "He's saying something."

"Very well, Miss Morris. But I will be back, I can promise you that. Hopefully next time, you will cooperate more easily than your daughter did."

"Get out!" Aunt Veronica roared. "Now." A ripple of energy pulsed through the shop. Dishes rattled. Papers fluttered. The hanging chandelier flickered, swaying back and forth on its chain. We watched, open-mouthed and a little terrified.

"This isn't the last you've seen of me." The man warned before turning to the door. "You'll come to regret this decision." With that, he replaced his hat and stomped out the door, the bell jangling in his wake.

We looked at one another. Even Albus seemed to have lost his fight. Slowly, we creaked open the door a bit further to peek out. Veronica leaned over the counter, shoulders rising and falling with heavy breaths. The quake in the shop settled, the lights stabilized once more.

"...Mom?" Emily's soft voice came from the top of the stairs. She crept down one step at a time. All stood silent save for the creaking of the stairs.

Aunt Veronica didn't look up. Maybe she couldn't hear us. Maybe she was too lost to herself.

Emily reached the landing and crept over to the desk. Aunt Veronica still braced herself against the wood tabletop, seething.

"Mom?"

It wasn't until Emily was right in front of her that she reacted. She looked up. Blinked. Shook her head.

"Oh," she whispered. "Emily. I'm sorry."

Emily rushed around the desk and embraced her mother. The stress seemed to flow out of the both of them, dissipating into the air.

"I'm sorry you had to see that," Veronica said, still holding her daughter. "But you know I won't let that man or anyone else hurt you again."

"When you talked about coming back with a warrant, that made me think. There's something that doesn't make sense in all of this." I approached the desk. "The Paranormal Enforcement Agency is known for its strict rules and guidelines. They normally have paper trails a mile long. Remember all the forms we had to fill out for our witch's license, Emily?"

"Yeah, now that you mention it." She perked up. "It actually fits with what I was telling you, Kat." She pulled away, looked up at her mother, then at me. "I don't think that's the real PEA."

The thought had crossed my mind, but it sounded so crazy, too out there to be true. Then again, Haven had seen its fair share of imposters lately.

"I don't get it," I thought aloud. "If they're not actually with the PEA, then what are they doing here? And what do they want?"

Emily shook her head. "I don't know, but I want to find out — starting with this little gadget right here." She held up the tracking device.

Aunt Veronica frowned. "You better not be getting yourself in even more trouble. I don't like this at all."

"Neither do I," Emily agreed. "Which is why Kat and I have a plan."

We do?

Veronica rubbed her hands together, pulled her hair up into a ponytail, then slumped into a chair. With one hand on the chair arm and the other bracing her forehead, she said, "I hope you know what you're doing."

"Why do you think I went digging through all dad's old stuff? I knew it was too dangerous to go snooping through in person. This will allow us to observe from a distance and get all the information we need."

"Dad what?" With that, the door opened, and in stepped my uncle.

"Oh, there you are, Ben." Aunt Veronica put her hands on her hips and observed her husband. "Our daughter is back, only to have some kind of wild ideas about going back into the belly of the beast. She gets it from you — look, she's even dug up one of your old toys."

Uncle Ben noticed the contraption in Emily's hands and immediately brightened. "Whoa, where did you find that thing? It's been ages — never did figure out what happened to it."

I strained not to roll my eyes. Emily was more used to his antics, though. "It was in a weird compartment at the bottom of one of your bookshelves. Were you trying to hide it or something? Cause that's sure what it felt like."

"Oh, jeez. That's where it was?" He smacked a hand to his head. "I must have hidden it there when Bobby kept asking me to borrow it. You remember Bobby..."

"Both of you, shush." Aunt Veronica spoke over both of them. "This is all fine and good, but this isn't a game. There are very serious matters to discuss here. I think everyone needs to be on the same page."

I held up my hands. "That's fair, that's fair."

"Ben, go lock up. The rest of you, follow me."

"Where are we going?" We headed down the hallway toward the living quarters and up the stairs to the second floor.

Aunt Veronica bounded into the kitchen with determination. "Far be it from me to let anyone fight crime on an empty stomach."

CHAPTER EIGHTEEN

Eating a kitchen witch's cooking is something everyone should do at least once. There's a reason I often preferred holidays at my aunt's house rather than my mother's.

The food was absolutely spectacular, imbued with a magical touch only certain witches could provide. That didn't mean the meal was a lighthearted family affair, though.

Aunt Veronica got down to business as soon as we all sat down at the table. We discussed the competition in great detail, the events leading up to Fabio's death, and the days Emily had spent in isolation. Talk soon moved to theories about the PEA's involvement and the presence of them in Buried Treasure this very evening.

With so much at stake, the decision was clear:

the PEA wouldn't be able to help us. The Haven police weren't equipped to deal with magical crime. Even if they were, revealing our powers would do more harm than good.

So where did that leave us? You guessed it. It was up to us.

I could tell my aunt and uncle weren't happy about us going back to the scene, but this was our chance to make things right. This was our chance to finally find some answers. So after we finished dinner and cleaned the dishes, Em and I laid down for a short nap.

We had a long night ahead of us, and we needed all the energy we could get.

After a few hours of sleep and a full belly, we prepared for the night's outing.

"Is sneaking out in the middle of the night some new trend?" Albus asked, weaving between our legs. "Cause y'all sure have been doing it a lot lately."

He had a point, albeit an awkward one. "Guess we have been pretty busy," I mused. "But it always pays off in the end."

"I hope it does this time," Emily said. She hoisted

the car under one arm and slung a pack over her other shoulder. "You ready?"

"As I'll ever be." With goodbyes and well-wishes from both my aunt and uncle, we strode out the door and toward the next phase of our mission.

The night stood cold and welcoming. I didn't mind the chill in the air — it made me feel alive. Kept me awake. Kept me focused. Tonight, as we drew near the competition site once more, we had a plan.

Emily and I would keep watch at a distance, while we set the tracker to explore each of the bakers' stations. Albus would prowl the perimeter as a scout. All we had to do was get in, get the readings, get out.

At least, that was the plan.

And you know what they say about best-laid plans.

We weren't far from the competition site when we heard a voice out of the darkness. I acted fast, ducking behind a nearby tree. Albus and Emily followed suit. Adrenaline pumped through my veins and clouded my thoughts as I tried to listen.

There wasn't supposed to be anyone else out there. That's why we came this late at night.

That wasn't even the worst of it, though.

"I'm telling you, I have it under control."

There was that all-too-familiar voice again. I couldn't hear anyone else respond — perhaps he was on the telephone?

"Don't worry, they don't suspect a thing." A pause. "No, that won't be necessary."

Emily clenched my hand in a crushing grip. I held my breath, listening for more.

"I'll let you know if anything changes. Just keep them off my back a little longer." Footsteps. "Very well. Goodbye."

I didn't dare say anything, but my mind raced with the new information. I clung to the tree and listened as the footsteps grew further away. Only after they faded away did I unclench my muscles.

"Was that..." Emily whispered, her voice tight.

"Looks like our agent has a few more secrets to hide," I replied. "I think he's gone. Let's go do what we came to do and get out. This place gives me the creeps."

"Amen to that," Emily agreed.

I peeked out from behind the tree slowly at first. I kept my movements quiet, just in case.

The field was empty once more, save for the yellow tape and the baking stations. They still stood there even days later, untouched, like some kind of gravestone frozen in time. Would they ever move them? Even I didn't know.

Emily and I stood at the taped perimeter while Albus sniffed around. She sat down the tracker, pressed a button on the underside, and closed her eyes. Laying a hand on the topside panels, she whispered a word and released a tendril of white light. It absorbed into the panel and dissolved.

Then the car began to move.

It crept along slowly at first, pointing its sensors this way and that. It let out a small beep and sped up, heading straight for Emily's station. At least, the one she'd been reassigned after the twist.

"Look," I pointed. "You might be on to something after all."

With a series of robotic beeps and boops, it paused right in front of the cooking station. A green light flashed on its front.

"What's it saying?" I asked Emily.

"Dunno," she replied. "Can't tell from here. We can recall it and look at the recordings."

"Okay. Do it. Hurry."

Emily clicked a small button in her hand and made a waving gesture. The mechanical tracker, as if hearing her, turned and started to rumble back toward us.

"Well, that was easy," Albus observed. "And apart

from the early panic, seems to have gone off without a hitch."

Suddenly, a twig cracked behind us. We spun around in unison to see the last person I expected.

Ginger Ardice threw her hands up, frozen into a shocked deer-in-the-headlights gaze.

"What are you doing here?" We both said in unison.

Ginger kept her hands raised. "I don't mean any harm. I can explain, I promise!"

"Go on..." Emily said, holding the tracker close to her chest. Albus arched his back and bared his teeth.

"Putting aside the issue of why *you're* here in the first place..." Ginger started, finally putting her hands down. "I have a reason. Do you?"

I glanced at Emily. I didn't want to give away our plans, especially to someone who could be a suspect. "Let's talk," I proposed. "The three of us. But first, let's get away from here."

"Not yet." Ginger pointed past the tape into the competition area. "I'm looking for something I lost. That's why I came back to look for it."

"And what's that?" I crossed my arms.

"The memory card for my camera." She reached into her bag and pulled out a camera, not unlike the one I'd seen Jack using. "See?" Ginger popped open a compartment on the side, showing that it was empty.

"I was switching them out during the day of the competition and I guess I dropped it somewhere. I really need to find it before I go back home." She looked up at us with mournful eyes. That, I hadn't expected.

"I promised." Her shoulders slumped. "I keep coming back and combing the area, hoping I missed something, but...I can't find it."

"What does it look like?" I leaned in closer, trying to see the camera in the darkness. I had a general idea from working with Jack, but he also taught me there were many different kinds and brands of photo equipment, all with their own set of parts and pieces.

"It's about the size of a postage stamp. Rectangle. If you can help me find it I'll tell you everything I know. Promise."

"Why is it so important?" I wondered.

"Well," she shuffled her feet. "Let's go look. We can talk while searching."

I shrugged. "Fair enough. You okay with this, Em?" I looked over to my cousin. This was all her idea, after all.

"Sure. Let's find this thing and get out of here."

"So, my parents love to travel," Ginger started. We

swept the lights from our phones over the grass, looking for the memory card. "They were so proud of me when they found out I'd been selected as a competitor. They were planning to come with me, in fact."

"What happened?" Emily asked.

"Right before I was due to head out, they..." Ginger stopped for a moment. "Well, they got sick. It was real sudden. Out of nowhere. I didn't know what to do."

"Whether to stay with them or continue with the competition, you mean." I filled in the gaps. "That would be a difficult choice for anyone to make. I take it you chose the latter, though. Since you're here."

"I didn't want to, you know." Ginger frowned. "I told them I wanted to stay and take care of them, but they wanted me to pursue my dream." She sniffed. "The doctors are taking good care of them, but I still wish I was there."

I nodded in understanding. "Have you been able to stay in touch?"

"Yeah, every day." She held out her phone and waved it at me. "We do video chats every night before bed. There's one thing they wanted more than anything, though. When I came here."

"What's that?" Emily asked.

Ginger held up the camera. "For me to take

pictures here in Haven and bring them home."

Oh. Suddenly it all made sense why she was so determined to find that memory card. Her parents were in what could be their last days, and they wanted to vicariously travel one more time. Who could say no to a request like that?

"We'll do your parents proud," I promised. "There are more than a few savvy photographers here in town. How would you like a curated scrapbook by the locals?"

Ginger's face lit up, a genuine smile showing for the first time that night. "That would be amazing."

"I hoped you'd say that."

"Guys, I think I found something!" Emily called out from a few yards away. We whipped our heads around to face her. She punched her arm into the air in triumph. "Is this what you're looking for?"

Ginger rushed over and plucked it from Emily's hands. "It is! You found it!" She squealed with delight before fumbling the compartment on the camera back open. The card clicked into place and she let out an audible sigh of relief.

"Thank you *so* much," Ginger gushed. "Where did you find it? I could have sworn I picked over every square inch at least twice."

"It was pressed into the ground over there like someone stepped on it. There was a little bit of mud on top, but I caught a glint of it in the moonlight. Would have missed it otherwise."

"I hope it still works." Ginger flicked on the camera and peered at the screen. The backlight illuminated her tense expression. When the grid of photos started to crawl across the screen, she let out an even bigger sigh. "It does."

"Looks like luck's on your side tonight." I nudged her with a smile. "Let's not wear it out. Come on, let's get out of here."

"And go where?" asked Emily.

I tapped my chin in thought. "Who's up for a midnight snack?"

Even Albus took note of that one. "The diner?" Emily asked. "But what are we going to do with..." she gestured at the tracker.

"We'll keep it in my trunk while we eat, then decipher the clues back at your place. Deal?"

"Deal."

Emily, Albus, and I started heading for my car, but Ginger hung back. "We did something for you, now you're gonna do something for us," I called over my shoulder and waved for Ginger to come along. "You're coming too."

Ginger jogged to meet up with us. Soon we were all piled into my car, heading to the best — and only — late-night diner in town.

CHAPTER NINETEEN

The Midnight Diner was the kind of place you went when you didn't want to be bothered. It stayed open twenty-four hours, kept the coffee coming, and the wait staff was about as unobtrusive as they came.

In other words, perfect for our little discussion.

The diner sat eerily empty this time of night. Soft jazz tunes played from a jukebox in the back corner and a ceiling fan turned lazily. The sounds of fat sizzling on the flat-top and the steady ticks of the old grandfather clock completed the ambiance.

We got seated at a small, secluded table near the back. It was the one closest to the jukebox, which meant it would be even harder to eavesdrop. I ordered each of us a cup of coffee and while the waitress went to fetch it, I folded my hands and looked across the table at my companions. Albus curled up in my bag between my feet, after much complaining about the "undignified" treatment.

"So," I began.

"So," Ginger repeated.

"Let's start with why you were at the scene in the middle of the night," Emily started. She took a sip of the steaming coffee and winced at the temperature, nearly spilling it down her shirt.

"I told you. I was looking for my camera card."

"In the middle of the night?" Emily furrowed her brow. "You could have easily waited until morning. Would be a lot easier to see once the sun came up."

"I was just so nervous," Ginger said. She stirred one packet of sugar into her coffee while staring off into space. Then another. She was on a third packet when she realized what she was doing. "See? My mind's been a mess ever since the incident."

"Uh-huh...I'm not buying it." Emily crossed her arms. "What do you think, Kat?"

Great. I hated being put on the spot like this. I glanced between Emily and Ginger. They both had their reasons, but I had to admit Ginger's excuse was pretty weak.

"Are you sure there's not anything else?" I asked. If Emily was going to be the bad cop in this scenario, I'd have to be the good one. "We're trying to figure this out, same as you. The more information we can share with one another, the better off we'll be."

Ginger was silent a moment as if considering this. Finally, her face softened. "Okay. That's not the only reason." She dug into her pocket and pulled out a crumpled receipt, pushing it across the table to us. "I found this."

I smoothed it out between Emily and me so we could both read it. The moment I saw the words, I drew in a sharp gasp.

This receipt was from a library, for a very particular book —

Fierce Accidents: Wonders of the Great Dark Arts.

"See!" Emily squeaked a little too loudly. "It *was* a dark curse!"

"Shh!" Ginger and I both hissed at once. Emily drew back into herself, mouthing an apology.

"Where did you find this?" I asked Ginger. I tried to make out the name of the library, the patron's name, or any other identifying information, but it had already rubbed away — lucky for them, yet another obstacle for us.

"It was in the common area back at the bed and breakfast." Ginger said. "I saw it when I was looking for my memory card. Thought it was just a piece of trash at first — then I noticed the title written on it."

"Good thing you didn't throw it away," I said. "Looks like we have another clue."

"It could be nothing." Ginger shrugged. "I don't know how many people come and go at the Starlight, but I'm sure it's a lot. More than just us, that's for sure. It could be from anyone. And even so, checking out a book on dark magic is hardly a crime in itself."

"True," I conceded. "But it's a bit too much of a coincidence, don't you think?"

"It's something to keep an eye on," Emily admitted. "I'd like to see the readings from the tracker bot before we make any wild assumptions."

"Fair enough," I agreed.

Before we could dig any deeper into the topic, the waitress came back with our food — pancakes for Ginger and me, an omelet for Emily.

We spent the next few minutes digging in. Investigating a crime, after all, was hungry work. I even managed to slip a few morsels down to Albus, who sat dutifully between my legs. As I ate, I thought about the clue Ginger had shared with us.

It could give us the boost we needed to crack the case, or it could be a cold red herring. I wanted to share with her my own suspicions about the PEA and Emily's experience with them, but I still wasn't sure.

Ginger seemed like a good enough person, but

she was still a suspect. Should we give her even more information? I was trying to figure out how to ask Emily this privately when Ginger slid out from the vinyl booth.

"If you'll excuse me, I've got to go to the bathroom. Where is it?"

I pointed it out and she scurried off, leaving the two of us at the table, alone.

"Talk about timing," Emily spoke up first.

"Yeah, tell me about it. You thinking the same thing I am?"

"I don't know how much to tell her."

"Neither do I." I chewed my lip in thought, weighing the options. "She's been a big help to us, and her alibi seems genuine, but..."

"But..." Emily prompted. "She could be making it all up. People do that, you know. Make up these huge elaborate stories. Whole identities, even. What if we're playing right into her hands?"

I leaned forward, resting my chin on my fist. "I don't know, Em. I just don't know."

I didn't have much more time to think about it, either, because Ginger came back from the bathroom and slid into the booth across from us once more.

"What'd I miss?" She asked, flicking her gaze between the two of us.

I pressed my lips together. Hopefully, she hadn't heard us talking about her.

"Nothing much." Emily stepped in so I didn't have to. She angled her fork toward Ginger's plate. "How're your pancakes?"

"They're delicious." Ginger said, taking another big bite. "Really good. The malt mix makes a big difference."

"That's the secret ingredient," Emily winked. "Don't tell."

"So what about you two?" Ginger asked, undeterred. "I trusted you enough to share that receipt with you. Especially since, well...you're the one they're accusing."

Emily scowled. "You don't actually believe that nonsense, do you?"

"Would I be here if I did?" Ginger dug back into her pancakes without saying another word.

She had a point. We ate in silence for a few minutes more. Emily was the next one to speak, and when she did so, she no longer had the same accusatory tone.

"Look...I'm sorry, Ginger. For being suspicious, I mean. You saw how quickly they turned against me with hardly any evidence to go on. I'm just..." She bunched up the napkin in her hands. "I'm scared, I guess. Someone out there really did do this. Accident or not, there's powerful magic at work here. Not to mention the PEA are acting pretty suspicious, themselves." She sighed and dropped the napkin into her hap. "It's hard to know who to trust."

At length, Ginger nodded. "I understand," she started. "Really. I do — maybe not the being accused part, but I want to figure this out as much as you do." She frowned. "I have my own reasons. For one, they're not letting us go home until the case is closed."

"They?" I asked. I didn't need an answer — not really. I already knew who she was talking about.

"The PEA." She made air quotes with her hands. "I've never seen an agent act like that before, though."

"That's nothing," Emily said with renewed vigor. "Get a load of this..."

"Yeah, there's something fishy going on. That's for sure." Ginger leaned back in the booth and pushed her empty plate away before crossing her arms. The jukebox had flipped over to a selection of classic rock anthems now, the bass and drums thumping so loud it vibrated what little coffee was left in my mug. "But what can we do about it?"

"That's what we're trying to figure out," I said.

"This library receipt is a big help, though. With the information we picked up on the tracker, maybe we can make sense of all this."

"I sure hope so," Ginger said. "I want to go home." She frowned, her eyes glazed over with sadness. "I want to see my parents again."

"You will." I reached across the table and took her hand. It was a small gesture, but it seemed like she needed it. "I promise." I squeezed her palm gently, and she squeezed back.

With a yawn, Ginger slid out of the booth and stretched, looking down at us. "Thank you both, for listening to me. For believing me. I've got to get going — sleep is calling my name, but do reach out if you learn anything else. You know where to find me."

"We will," Emily said. "And I trust that you will do the same for us."

"Of course." She turned for the door after paying her bill and threw up a hand in farewell. "Take care, now."

"Y'all come back," muttered the woman at the register. She didn't even look up from her crossword puzzle.

"Looks like that's our cue." I had to suppress a yawn, myself. With Ginger gone, exhaustion finally caught up with me. I couldn't hold it back any longer.

I let out a big, mouth-wide-open yawn, which triggered Emily to do the same.

"Looks like it," Emily agreed. "Let's go home."

I peeked down at Albus. He had curled up in a small little circle, his head resting on my left foot. "What?" He mumbled sleepily.

"We're leaving. Wake up."

He moved slowly, stretching each limb and letting out a jaw-breaking yawn. "I was having the most wonderful dream..."

"And what's that?" I asked as I ushered him back into my bag.

"You know that fishing game you like to play on your tablet? It was real! So many fish...so yummy..."

Yup. He was definitely still half asleep.

CHAPTER TWENTY

By the time Emily and I got back to her house, I could barely keep my eyes open. I had to carry my cat inside — he didn't even wake when I pulled him out of the car.

"I know you want to look at the tracker, but I'm beat." Emily opened the door and let her bag drop to the floor. "See you in the morning?"

I didn't have the energy to resist. "Yeah. Something like that."

Technically, it was already morning. Technically, I didn't care. I collapsed into the guest bed without bothering to change. I was asleep before my head hit the pillow.

I dreamed about a little black cat and a witch on a broomstick, zipping through the sky.

It wasn't a lot of sleep, but I didn't feel like I was

about to fall over anymore.

I woke before Emily. When I peeked into her room, she was still snoring away.

I decided to use this opportunity to check out the tracker. Sitting down on the living room floor, I pulled the small car into my lap. "Let's see what you can tell us," I muttered.

Honestly, I didn't know if it would do anything at all. My heart started pounding. What if the thing never woke up? What if I had to wait for it to recharge or something?

Emily was the one running this thing, after all. Not me. I found a switch buried in the undercarriage and flicked it on.

Nothing happened.

Well, that wasn't quite true. Something did happen. The panels up top flashed blue, bright enough to hurt my eyes. Then it died.

"Hey!" I whined. "What did I do?"

Looked like I spoke too soon. Light spilled out once more, protecting a hologram-like image on the living room floor.

I gasped, watching the image play out. It was like a heat map of the competition area. Squares represented each of the baking stations, and a rectangle represented the judging table.

One station, in particular, lit up brighter than the

others. I squinted and looked closer. Sure enough, it was Emily's station.

"Whoa."

I looked up and saw Emily standing in the hallway, staring at the image.

"What happened?" she asked.

"I don't know—" I started.

"Oh, wait! It's finished rendering!"

I looked back at the hologram. Indeed, it had changed. Sharpened. A pulse blipped out from the station in question, radiating outward in concentric circles. A reading appeared in scrolling text above the image:

> aberrant magic detected - concentration: high.

Emily gasped and leaned in closer.

"What does that mean?" I asked, suddenly wishing I'd paid more attention to magical engineering class.

"That there is definitely a curse present...but it's only present in this one area." She pointed. "The station I ended up at."

And to think, things would have gone very differently if only they'd kept their original stations...

"Do you think someone meant for you to get that station?" I mused. My stomach clenched at the thought of it. "Do you think that's why they had a last-minute switch?"

"Could be." Emily considered. "Or it could just be a coincidence."

"Well, regardless if it was intentional or not, that station was definitely cursed. The only question now, is why?" I rubbed my chin with one hand and stroked Albus' fur with the other. "Were they trying to harm the baker...or the judges?" I looked at the image again then back to Emily. "Everyone at the tournament was from out of town, except for you. Right?"

"Right."

"You didn't know any of the competitors or judges beforehand?"

"Nope," Emily replied. "I mean, I'd heard of some of the judges, but no, I didn't have any kind of personal relationship with them. No reason for anyone to have it out for me if that's what you're suggesting."

"Hmm." Something still didn't fit. The pieces were all here, laid out in front of us. But like a frustrating jigsaw puzzle, I couldn't figure out the pattern to link them all together. "Before everyone rotated," I started, another idea forming. "Who was at that station? Could the curse be intended for them instead?"

Emily thought for a moment. "Meryl. Meryl was there originally."

"Meryl," I muttered to myself. "And she had no shortage of enemies."

"You think someone was trying to curse her, instead?"

"It's not out of the realm of possibility." I shrugged. "But until we have more proof, that's all it is — just a speculation."

"We need to find out who borrowed that curse book," Emily suggested. "I bet if we can find them, we can figure out who cast the curse."

The hologram from the tracker flickered and went out. The motor powered down. "Hey, what happened?" I waved my hand across the space the image had been.

"Processing that data takes a lot of energy," Emily explained. She scooted over next to me and picked it up out of my lap, peering at something on the underside. "Yeah, it needs to recharge. We got what we needed, though."

"Did we?" I sighed and leaned back against the couch, staring at the ceiling. "Feels like we're right where we started."

"We will figure this out," Emily nudged me. "Or more likely, you will figure this out. You're Kat the super sleuth, remember?"

I snorted. "Yeah. No pressure." With a groan, I got back to my feet and looked at the clock. It would be time for work soon, and even though I so didn't feel like it, I couldn't afford to take another day off.

"Will I see you tonight at the piano recital?" Emily asked, changing the subject.

"What rec—*oh.*" I covered my face in my hands. My father finally had his first public gig tonight. It wasn't anything glamorous — just a small gathering at the community theater, but he was really excited. "I totally forgot. Wow. I feel like a terrible daughter now."

"I only just now remembered because my phone pinged me with a calendar event." She waved the screen at me. "But I wouldn't worry about it. We've both been through a lot lately. It's common to forget things in times of stress."

"Isn't that the truth." I stretched, yawned one more time, and walked to the door. Albus followed, for once not having anything snarky to say. "Well, I'll see you tonight." I gave her one last hug before heading out.

"Don't forget the rest of our crazy family," Emily reminded me, a grin growing across her face.

Oh right. My dad invited *everyone.*

"Like I could forget." I laughed and walked back to my car. Another day of work was ahead. Another day of questions without answers.

If I was so close to solving this mystery, why did I feel more lost than ever?

"Thanks again," the customer said on their way out the door. One down, a million more to go.

I turned to Jack, who was organizing things on the shelves out front. "How you doing out there?"

Jack wiped a sheen of sweat from his forehead. "I'm alive, aren't I?" He gave me a wink and wiped his hands on his apron. "It just feels like it's a hundred degrees in here."

"You know the plants have to have a certain temperature to thrive," I reminded him, pointing at the thermostat. "And it's hardly one hundred — it's set at a perfectly comfortable eighty-five degrees."

"Are you serious?" Jack glared at me. "That's way too hot for indoors."

"Hey, if you can't take the heat, get out of the greenhouse." I chuckled to myself at the joke. "Besides, what you're feeling is the humidity, not the heat. Usually, we have better ventilation, but it's been on the fritz the last few days and I haven't been able to get someone in to look at it. That's why it feels like a sauna in here."

"Ah," Jack replied. He hefted a box of excess

inventory and carried it past me to the stockroom. "Say," he called out from behind me. "How's that whole business with the poison pie going?"

Ah. That. "It's...going. That's about all the information I've got for you."

"I heard they suspected Emily." Jack frowned. "She wouldn't do anything like that. She would never..."

"I know," I said a little more forcefully than I intended. "You know that, I know that, the whole town knows that. But whoever's been crawling around town looking for clues doesn't."

"You mean the PEA?" He raised an eyebrow.

I bit my lip, wondering if I should tell him my theory. "Yes." I left it at that.

"Is there anything I can do to help?" He asked. "The sooner we get this solved, the sooner things can go back to normal."

Ha. Normal. What even was normal in this crazy town anymore? I was about to say no, then I remembered Ginger's request. I'd promised her a scrapbook of Haven, and here I was standing next to one of the town's best photographers. "Actually, there is one thing," I started. "It's not directly related to the case, but it would be a big help."

"What's that?"

"Can you send me a link to that online gallery of yours? I have a few photos I want to print..."

As the day wound down, I found myself thinking more and more about the evening's family gathering. Getting everyone together was always "fun", to say the least. So many clashing personalities made for an interesting time. Speaking of which, I hadn't seen my Grandma Crystal in some time. I wondered if she knew how to decipher the receipt. She'd helped us scry old notes in the past...maybe she had something to say about this one as well?

I texted Emily to make sure she'd taken a picture of the receipt. It wasn't as good as the real thing, but maybe we could still get something out of it.

Or maybe not. Still, it was worth a try.

I thanked Jack for his help, started packing up for the day, and double-checked the location of the night's recital. I'd need to go home and change out of my dirty work clothes, of course, but then I'd have to head right back out.

Maybe one day this century, I'd get a full night of sleep. Was that too much to ask?

CHAPTER TWENTY-ONE

By the time I arrived at the community theater that night, most of my family had already arrived.

It wasn't just my relatives, though — my dear mother had gone out of her way to invite everyone who would listen. The lobby was packed with chattering villagers. I pushed through the crowd, looking for my father.

I found him at the stage door, sipping a cup of water. His eyes darted this way and that. He bounced back and forth on the balls of his feet.

"Ah, there's my Kat," he said, extending his arms for a hug.

"Tonight's the big night, huh?"

My dad gave a nervous laugh. "Yeah, looks like it. I had no idea your mother invited so many people, though. It's not that big of a deal." He tossed the styrofoam cup into a nearby trashcan and rubbed the back of his neck. "What if I get up there and mess up in front of all these people? The whole town will be talking about it."

"Try not to think about it that way," I suggested, though I knew that was about as easy as telling the sun not to shine. "You've been practicing like crazy. I'm sure you'll do great."

"I hope so," he said, shoving his hands in his pockets. "I know I've been practicing and I know the pieces like the back of my hand, but there's always that fear."

"I know." Boy, did I ever. "But I wanted you to know I'm really proud of you, dad. For following your dream."

That lit him up. "Thanks, Kat. You and your mom have been my biggest supporters throughout. I wouldn't be here without you."

I returned his warm gesture. "Now go out there and break a leg — err, not literally." I winked.

"Not literally," he repeated. The clock struck the top of the hour and he waved goodbye before heading backstage. "See you after the show!"

"See you." I watched him go, a lightness in my heart contrasting with all the heavy drama of the last few days. Two years ago, my father retired. He'd always wanted to be a musician, but life had other plans for him. Now in retirement, he finally had a chance to pursue his dream. Tonight was his first public recital after years of practice, and I couldn't be more proud.

For now, all I had to do was rejoin the rest of my family and enjoy the show.

When I returned to the lobby everyone was heading to their seats. We had a reserved row to ourselves, right up front. I joined my mother, grandmother, aunt, and uncle there. Also in attendance were Emily and her brother Matt. Albus hadn't come along tonight — something about a hairball — but the rest of the Sullivan family was out in force.

My mom and grandma were already at it, of course — bickering over grocery brands, of all things — so I decided to sit next to Emily and Matt. Even though I'd spent plenty of time with Emily lately, I didn't have many chances to hang out with Matt.

"Long time, no see." He whispered, giving me a fist bump. "Was starting to think you were avoiding me just like Em here." He nudged her and chuckled.

"Am not!" Emily hissed.

"Are too," Matt shot back.

"It's not my fault I got caught in the middle of a murder mystery!"

"Hush!" My mom hissed at all three of us. "The show's about to start!"

This conversation, such as it was, would have to wait. The curtain rose, the lights went down, and the audience grew quiet. My father sat alone in front of a grand piano up on the stage, the spotlights all aimed at him.

All was silent. All was still. Then he began to play.

Music floated throughout the hall, filling the theater and bouncing off the walls. As the notes turned into bars and bars into a song, the music took me back, all the way to when I was a child.

You know how they say smells can trigger certain memories? Well, sounds can too. The piano music took me back to a time when life was simpler. A time with fewer responsibilities, less stress, and definitely no looming murder cases.

Grandma Crystal had come over to celebrate Samhain with us, and she'd brought presents. I remembered that part especially — what child doesn't like presents? It was the nature of that gift that stood out to me, though, as I sat there in the auditorium and watched my father perform.

It was an enchanted toy, which wasn't so unusual, but as she sat it on the ground in front of Matt, Emily, and me, it changed. When I touched it, it turned my favorite color — green — and bounced around me in circles, leaving child me chasing after it with shrieks of joy.

The same toy turned pink for Emily, floating through the air like a butterfly for her to catch. Matt got purple and it started climbing the walls, the furniture, and the ceiling in some kind of twisted toy parkour.

"How does it do that?" I remember my mom asking as she watched us play.

"It's a special kind of adaptive magic," Grandma Crystal replied. "Some say it's a dark spell, but just because they came up with it doesn't mean we can't have a little fun."

"Mom!" my mother hissed. I remembered staring up at them as the toy rolled and changed and morphed around us. "Are you sure it's safe to have around the children?"

"It's fine," Grandma Crystal promised. "Magic isn't inherently light or dark. It's what we do with it that matters. And look at them — aren't they happy?"

The toy zoomed past me and flickered colors again. My easily-distractible brain forgot all about the grownups and chased after it once more, lost to the innocent bliss of childhood.

That was it, I realized as I sat there in the front row. That was the key I'd been missing. I wanted to leap up and test my theory right away, but then I remembered where I was.

It was family memories that gave me the insight I so desperately needed. And here, tonight, I would make some new family memories — but only if I was present, body and mind.

So I put those worries away — as best I could, anyway — and listened to the swell of the music. At the end of the day, it all came down to family, didn't it?

I glanced to each side of me. Matt, Emily, my uncle, my mom, my grandma. They'd all been there for me during different parts of my life. And with each case I faced and each problem I solved, I never did it alone.

I had my team. I had my family. And as crazy as they drove me sometimes, I wouldn't trade them for the world.

After the performance, the immediate family agreed to meet back at my mom's house for a reception of sorts. I know it wasn't that big of a concert or anything, but it was something of a summation of my dad's efforts and dreams. He'd put his mind to learning piano and finally achieved his goal of playing in front of an audience. We wanted to make it as special a day for him as possible.

On the way over to my mom's house, I had time to think things through in the car. If I could get my grandma alone for a few minutes, I wanted to ask her about the receipt Em and I found.

Alone was the key word, though. I didn't need my mom snooping into our business — more than she already did, that is. If I didn't know better, I would say snooping was her middle name.

So when we got to the house, the first thing I did was pull Emily out onto the back patio.

"What?" She asked when the sliding door closed behind us.

"You still have the pics of the curse book receipt that Ginger showed us?"

Emily fished into her pocket, swiped through a few screens on her phone, and held it up to show me. "Right here. Are you thinking what I'm thinking?"

"It's as good a time as any, right? Everyone's already here in one place."

She faltered for a moment, leaning over the railing to look up at the clear night sky. "I know this is supposed to be your dad's big night...but I can't stop thinking about it, either."

I frowned but nodded in agreement. "Yeah. I don't exactly feel great about it, but it's not like we're flat out ignoring him. I don't see why we can't spend time, hang out, mingle for a bit then drift off to do our own thing."

"Deal." Emily pocketed her phone and slid open the patio door, beckoning for me to follow. "Now come on, before your mom notices we're gone. We'll never hear the end of it!"

A few (well, maybe more than a few) glasses of wine later, we were all sprawled comfortably across the couch, chairs, and cushions in the living room. The TV played some old movie that no one was watching, and my dad had fallen asleep slumped over in his chair.

I thought about waking him so he could go to bed properly, but I decided against it. He'd had a long day. I'd let him rest a little longer. When my mom got up to go to the bathroom, I gestured to Emily. It was time for us to take a chance.

"Hey, Grandma?" I asked, trying to sound as innocent as I could. "Could you come outside with me for a moment?"

"Well, sure," she started. "But why? What's outside?"

I lowered my voice and drew in closer. "Em and I were planning a surprise for mom's birthday, but we don't want her to know about it. That's why we waited till she went to the bathroom to ask you."

Grandma Crystal's eyes lit up. "You have my attention." She said, getting up from her chair. We didn't have to say another word — she was already on her way to the door. "You know I can't turn down a good surprise. Come on, let's chat out here before your mother gets back."

Emily raised a questioning eyebrow at me. I winked, she mouthed an "oh", and we followed her out.

"Now what's this all about?" She asked, rubbing her hands together. "I haven't had a chance to surprise my daughter in ages."

There was one problem with my brilliant plan. I hadn't actually thought about what the surprise would actually *be*.

"We, um..." I dragged out my words and hoped for more time. "We haven't ironed out a lot of the details yet because we know how much you love surprises, so we thought you could help us brainstorm."

Whew, saved.

"Oh, that's a good idea," Grandma Crystal agreed, putting a hand to her chin. "A party would be nice. You know how she loves being the center of attention."

"We all know," I quipped. I didn't mean it in a rude way — was just a statement of fact.

"I'll get to thinking," she said excitedly. It was honestly kind of adorable. Grandma Crystal bounced up and down, the previous tiredness all but forgotten. What could I say? It was infectious. I felt myself getting riled up too, and this wasn't even the reason we came out here in the first place!

I reigned back in my focus and nudged Emily. "There was something else we wanted to ask you about too, but it's of a...different topic."

"Oh?" Her eyebrows raised past the rim of her oversized glasses.

I had no idea how to broach the topic, so I launched right into it. "Remember when you helped Pepper and I decipher that note we found in Starla's shop?"

"Yes..." she started, but her face grew more serious this time. "Don't tell me you've been snooping around again."

"Um," I winced. "Maybe?"

Her face broke out into a mischievous smile. "That's my granddaughter." She beamed and nudged me. "What's the latest dirt?"

"Wait...you're actually cool with it?" Emily stared at us in awe. "I thought you were going to give us a talking to like our moms did."

Grandma Crystal made a dismissive gesture. "Ah, where's the fun in that? And besides, you've helped solve the last two cases, haven't you? Clearly, you've got a good head on your shoulders."

I probably shouldn't be excited that my grandmother was encouraging illegal activity such as interfering with law enforcement. Probably. But everyone else gave us such a hard time about it — for good reason, I knew — it was nice to have someone in our corner.

"We found this and think it might be a clue." Emily handed the phone over to Grandma Crystal. "But we can't tell who borrowed the book or from where. Thought maybe you'd have some extra insight."

She pressed her glasses further up her nose, squinting at the screen. "You know there's not much I can do with a digital image. I need the physical object to really detect the essence of a thing."

Emily's face fell. "So there's nothing you can do?"

"I didn't say that." She narrowed her eyes and let out a long breath. Looking at the image again, her eyes widened. "Hey, I know that book."

"You do?" Emily and I both said in unison.

"Why yes," she said. "It's the same book I used to learn how to make those toys for you when you were kids."

My mouth dropped open. I blinked. "Wait...are you sure? *This* book? It's a curse book, why would you..."

"A good witch knows when to test the rules," her eyes glittered. "And when to break them."

"Don't tell me you dabbled in dark magic," Emily gasped.

"You must remember, darling," Grandma Crystal said. "There is no such thing as dark and light magic. It's all a give and take of energy, at the end. It's how we direct those energies that counts."

"That doesn't really answer my question, though." Emily frowned. "If this is the same book you used to learn those charms, then couldn't someone else use that same magic for curses? Specifically...a curse such as what happened at the competition?"

"Hmm, now that you mention it...it's possible. Only, it would manifest in a very different way, of course. What you didn't know, when I enchanted those toys for y'all, was that there are two sides to every coin. I chose to use my magic to make it appeal to your favorite colors and activities, remember?"

"I remember," I said fondly. "I always thought that was such a cool trick."

"But think about it this way — what if that same structure was used to root out a person's weaknesses instead? What if it delved into the tiny little flaws in their magic, in their process, and magnified them?"

And there it was. The missing piece. The final key.

Emily and I gawked at one another, coming to the same conclusion at the same time.

It was time to go back to the Starlight. Time to see if my hunch was correct.

CHAPTER TWENTY-TWO

We slept over at my mom's place that night. The wine and late hour wore on us, and soon enough we were all fast asleep.

The morning came earlier than I would have liked, but that was my own fault. As I woke and shook the cobwebs out of my brain, I thought about Albus.

He could take care of himself just fine, but I still wanted to stop by home and check on him for a bit before I headed in to work.

Downing a huge glass of water and willing my wine-induced headache to go away, I said my goodbyes and drug myself out the door to my car.

Albus, as expected, was at the door the moment I unlocked.

"Kat! Kat! Guess what!" He bombarded me as soon as I got inside.

"What..." I mumbled. It was too early for his level of energy.

"While you were gone last night and left me *all alone*, I got cold! My little cat bed wasn't cutting it, so I had to improvise..." He trotted toward the living room and checked over his shoulder every few steps, just to make sure I was watching.

I followed with apprehension. Any time Albus was excited to show me something, it was never a good sign. What kind of mischief had he gotten into this time?

It took all I had to keep from bursting out laughing. He'd dragged every blanket and pillow from my bed, piling them up into a kitty pillow fort of epic proportions. The blankets were arranged just so in a perfectly circular pattern. A warm, comfy area in the middle was flattened while my nice feather pillows surrounded it on all sides.

I put a hand to my mouth, unable to hide my smile. "Albus...what did you..."

"I can see why you humans love this stuff," Albus said proudly. He leaped into the pile and snuggled up, burrowing his head under the blanket and popping out the other side. "It's sooo comfy!"

"Albus..." I started. "That's my bedding! What am

I supposed to sleep on now?" I peeked into the bedroom just to check, and yup — the mattress was completely bare.

"I don't know, but you're not getting these back," Albus mumbled sleepily. "You've been holding out on me, Kat." He yawned as wide as his jaw would let him. "Now this is the life."

Okay, I couldn't help it. I laughed.

"What am I gonna do with you, silly cat." I watched him and shook my head.

"I don't know...love me?"

I sighed. "If I have to." Rolling my eyes, I went back to the bedroom. Looked like I needed a new set of sheets.

Once I had the bedroom re-situated, I looked at my watch and winced. It was nearly time for work already, and I still had questions nagging at the back of my mind. I had planned to go to the Starlight before work, but the little Albus incident had taken its place. Now I had a choice to make.

Could I get the job done in little enough time that Jack could watch the store in my stead? He'd done it before, and I knew he was good for it, but I hated leaving him alone. More than that, I hated leaving my stock unattended.

I pondered for a moment and made up my mind. Pulling out my phone, I dialed Jack's number. He should be just arriving at The Curious Cauldron if he wasn't there already.

"Hey, Jack?" I said when his voice came on the line.

"Yeah, what's up?"

"Think you could open up today? I have a, um, errand I need to run first. I'll be in a bit later."

A pause. "Sure, I can do that. Is everything all right?"

"Yeah, no problems here."

He didn't sound convinced. "Kat, you're not chasing a criminal again, are you?"

I opened my mouth to retort, then closed it. Was I that predictable? "Um...no?" I lied through my teeth.

"Kat," Jack said again, his voice a scathing monotone. "Lie a little better next time."

Ouch.

"Be careful out there. I'll see you when you get in." With that, Jack hung up.

I let out a breath and my arms fell to my sides.

"Well," I said to myself. "That could have gone better." On the plus side, though, Jack hadn't totally told me off or refused to cover for me. Small victories.

"He's right, you know." Albus' voice came muffled from underneath my blankets. "You really are terrible at lying."

"I didn't ask for comments from the peanut gallery!" I hissed. Walking over, I yanked the blankets off of him. He looked up with such hurt in his eyes you'd think I'd starved him for a week. "Now shush, we need to go."

"Go where?" Albus whined. "I was just getting comfortable."

"Clearly," I snarked back. "From the looks of it, you've been getting 'comfortable' the whole time I was gone. Now get up, we have work to do."

"Fine, fine," Albus growled and crawled out of his bed, shaking himself awake. "So bossy."

"Oh, like you've never been bossy with me." I teased him.

"Me?" He said in mock offense. "I would never."

"That's what I thought."

We arrived at the Starlight not long afterward. Albus trotted alongside me as I approached the counter, dinging the shiny silver bell there.

Ronnie came out of the back almost immediately, wiping his hands on a towel. "Ah, Kat! Good to see ya again. How can I help ya today?"

"I'm looking for Coral. Is she around?"

He furrowed his brow. "No. I'm afraid ya just

missed 'er. Left early this morning, in quite a rush, too."

I sucked in a breath. "Any idea where she might have gone?"

Ronnie shrugged. "She was goin' on about Piney Point, but I didn't catch much of it. Didn't ask — not my place. Why, she leave somethin' behind?"

"Something like that." I frowned. "Thank you for the information. We'll be going now."

"But ye only just arrived!" He called after us, but we were already out the door.

"So that happened," Albus said when we got back to the car. "What do we do now?"

"Sounds like she's on the run," I said breathlessly. "You know no one was supposed to leave yet."

"Wasn't she interested in the case as well?" Albus offered. "She asked us to check up on Meryl, remember?"

"You're right," I realized. "What happened to Meryl, anyway?"

"Dunno."

I sighed and started up the car. "One thing at a time, I guess."

Albus looked up at me from the passenger seat. "You sure about this, Kat?"

There was a loaded question if I'd ever heard one. "Yeah," I said at last, letting out a long breath.

"I'd feel better if you took someone with you." Albus licked at his paw and tilted his head. "Besides me, I mean. It could be dangerous, and there's only so much I can do if things go south."

"If Coral really is the culprit, she could be getting away as we speak." I knew Albus had a point, but I hardly had the time to drag someone else along with me. Emily would be at work by now too, and her job was a lot less forgiving than mine.

"Why don't you call that boyfriend of yours?" Albus said casually. "He's always helped you out of a jam before."

"I--" I started to correct him, but groaned. It wouldn't make a difference, he would tease me all the same. "I've been trying. I haven't heard from him, or any of the Wilders, since they left town. I'm getting worried."

"What was it you told me — one thing at a time?" Albus lay his head on his paws and curled his tail around himself.

"One thing at a time," I repeated to myself and put the car in drive.

Piney Point wasn't far, thank goodness. As we

drove, I had flashbacks to doing this same journey not so long ago. I'd had to chase down and confront Will McDaniel back then, and now it looked like I was about to do it all over again.

"Tell me again why we keep getting ourselves into these messes?" I said it more as a rhetorical question, but of course, Albus couldn't resist answering.

"Because you don't know how to keep your eyes on your own paper and have an overdeveloped sense of justice."

I snorted. "That's what we're calling it?"

"That's the nice way to put it."

We reached our destination about fifteen minutes later. I didn't see any other cars around, nor any other people. We couldn't have beaten her here — we left much later. Albus got out and ran around, trying to sniff for a scent. Nothing came up.

"Are you sure this is the right place?" He asked.

"That's what Ronnie said that she said." I shrugged. "Maybe she came and already left."

"Or maybe she was lying," Albus suggested. "So no one would know where she was actually going. Think about it, Kat. If she really was on the run, why would she tell someone where she was going?"

Yeah. Okay. That didn't make a lot of sense. But

here we were, so maybe we could find at least a little clue?

I walked further down the path before noticing a patch of crushed grass. Someone had stumbled through here, and recently. Following the trail, I ducked under the low-hanging branches and kept my eyes peeled. The sun couldn't pierce the dense canopy the further I got, draping the forest in cool, moist darkness.

I stopped when the trees opened up into a small clearing. Large, looming branches and growth still blocked out most of the light, but the ground cleared to a small circular area. I'd never seen anything like it before, and I'd been out here plenty of times.

"What do you think, Albus?" I turned around, but he wasn't there.

Wait...

"Albus?" I called, my voice shaking a bit.

No answer.

I readied my magic and scanned the area. At least out here in nature, I'd have an advantage as opposed to in the city.

Suddenly, I felt an arm around my neck. "You really fell for it. Didn't think you'd be so dense."

CHAPTER TWENTY-THREE

I froze in place the moment I heard that voice.

That was Coral.

"Let me go!" I hissed. "What are you doing?"

"No one can know what really happened," Coral said, her arm tightening against my neck. "It would ruin everything."

"What are you talking about?" I spun a tale in my mind to keep her talking. As long as she was talking, I could ready my magic. And then maybe, if I was lucky, I could get her away from me.

Where are you, Albus? He'd been right behind me this whole time, and then disappeared. If Coral did something to him...

My right hand clenched into a fist, and through

it, I poured the energy of the earth. The ground shuddered and shifted beneath our feet. Thankfully, I was used to it as a side effect of my magic.

Double thankfully, Coral wasn't. She lost her balance for just long enough to loosen her grip on my neck and stumbled backward. That's all the advantage I needed. I threw my weight in that direction and pushed.

The small rumble from the earth magic she could have recovered from. But a strong push when she was already off-balance? That sealed the deal. Arms flailing, mouth agape in shock, she fell to the ground and landed butt-first. Her head snapped back, precariously close to a jutting boulder, but her hands caught her fall in time to keep from cracking her skull.

Which was well enough for me — I didn't want to kill her, just restrain her.

I tapped into the powers of the earth and felt them flowing through me. I breathed in the scent of dirt and leaves and moss. At the moment Coral hit the ground, I stretched out my fingers into a grasping motion and focused my attention on the tufts of stringy moss around her.

Like tiny little snakes, the tendrils of moss began to quiver at first, then *move*.

"Wait!" Coral yelped. She tried to clamber to her

feet, but it was too late. Sprigs of moss looped themselves over her arms and legs and dove back into the earth, effectively holding her down.

"Hey!" She yanked at the bonds but they held firm. "Y-you're an earth witch!"

"Figured that out?" I couldn't resist throwing a bit of snark in there. She started it, after all. "Now let's talk about this. What are you doing here? Why did you follow me?"

A high pitched hiss behind me caught my attention. I turned around just in time to see Albus lunging into the action. "Albus!" I yelled, holding up a hand. "Wait!"

He landed nimbly on all fours in front of Coral's prone body but didn't attack. He bared his teeth and let out a low growl, but obeyed.

"Where were you, Albus?"

"I'm so sorry, Kat. My foot dropped right into a hole of soft dirt and I couldn't move — there were dead leaves everywhere and I think I accidentally inhaled a spider!"

"Okay, okay." I motioned for him to stop. Now was not the time for one of his dramatic monologues.

"Are you talking to that cat?" Coral asked, looking down at Albus and then at me. "Or did I hit my head?"

"Don't try to change the subject," I snapped at Coral. "Talk."

"I can explain. I swear. At least, I can try to."

"Why should I listen to you?" I crossed my arms and looked down at the bound woman. "You attacked me!"

"Will you give me a chance to explain? It's not what you think, I promise."

I raised an eyebrow. "Okay...go on..."

Coral sighed. She yanked at her bonds again. I loosened them just a little as a sign of goodwill but didn't let her go. "My family," she started, "is very achievement-oriented." She gave a rueful laugh and shook her head. "That's a nice way of putting it. It's almost like they didn't care about me. Only what I could win. What I could accomplish."

I furrowed my brow. "What does that have to do with anything?"

"It means," she started, "that I was under a lot of pressure to perform. I never felt like I could earn their love, no matter how much I did or how many awards I won." Her face fell and when she met my eyes this time, they were shining with tears. "Do you know how hard that was for me?"

Her words struck a chord. I hadn't had the most satisfying childhood either, but never feeling loved — only used? I couldn't imagine. "That sounds terrible,"

I admitted. "But things went a lot further than that here. Killing someone? There's no excuse for that."

Coral yanked her right hand so hard it ripped free of the moss. She held it up to stop me, her face stricken. "Let me finish." She panted the words. "Please."

I glanced down at Albus, still standing at attention. We'd come this far. I gestured for her to continue.

"Everything I did," Coral recounted, "or rather, everything I didn't do, it felt like they were keeping a tally." Her lip quivered. "I just kept thinking that if I could do something right — if I could win — that would show them that I was worthy of their love."

"You *are* worthy," I interjected, perhaps a bit too forcefully. No matter what happened, she needed to know that. "You don't need your parent's approval, or anyone else's, to prove that. No trophy or award can tell you that. That comes from inside."

With that, the situation changed. I took mercy on her and loosened the bonds. Even went over and helped get her upright. She leaned against the nearby boulder, still looking up at me like I was some kind of ghost.

I had no desire to be cruel, but I did what I had to do to protect myself. Now things had calmed a bit and we were talking. I didn't want her to run off, of course, but loosening the bonds would be a show of goodwill. If my experience talking to Will had taught me anything, it was that the other person needed to feel safe if they were going to talk. They needed to feel heard. Feel cared about.

"That better?" I asked softly.

"Yeah," Coral said, rubbing her wrists. "Thanks."

"I don't want to hurt you," I promised her. "But I'm not going to let you hurt me or Albus, either."

"A truce, then," Coral proposed.

"Truce."

She let out a long sigh and leaned her head back against the boulder. Her eyes drifted upward, where slats of sunlight and sky were just visible through the trees.

The clearing was silent for the next few moments. Even Albus let down his guard a little bit. He returned to my side, knocking his head against my calves.

"It's hard, you know?" Coral continued her monologue at last. "After you hear the same things said about you over and over, you start to believe it yourself." She shrugged. "All I ever wanted was to make them happy. Was to make them proud. But I can't even do that."

Things were starting to fall into place, but I

needed to know more. "Is that why you joined the competition circuit?"

"Well, one of the reasons. I really do like baking." Her face twisted into a scowl for a split second. "Well, I did at first. Without all the pressure, I mean. It was fun. But then it became everything, and I didn't know how to get out."

I gave her a sympathetic smile. She'd been through a lot, that was for sure. But there was something I still didn't get. "What was this feud between you and Meryl?" I remembered all too well the confrontation we'd had in the Starlight and how certain she'd been that Meryl was the real culprit. Had that all been a distraction?

"I found out, quite by accident, that Meryl was having an affair with Fabio. Yes — the same man that fell dead. The famed celebrity chef and judge. I had my inklings that Meryl was using her relationship to get special treatment in the competitions. Every time, no matter what happened, she happened to magically win the day."

"Why didn't you say anything?" I asked. "If you were so sure she was cheating."

"I tried to," Coral said. "At least at first. What I didn't realize was how many people Meryl had in her pocket. She'd paid off everyone that mattered, all the top ranks. It didn't matter what I or anyone else said at that point. There was nothing I could do."

"Nothing except win," I pointed out. "And you took that desire to win a little too far, didn't you?"

"I never meant to kill anyone!" Coral yelped. She waved her hands frantically. "I swear!"

CHAPTER TWENTY-FOUR

Albus twitched at my side. I let out a breath. "Then what happened?"

"I was doing some research and I learned that there were spells that could make one's magic mess up just a little bit. Expose their mistakes. That's all I wanted to do, I promise. I wanted Meryl to screw up and embarrass herself, so I cursed her station. I wanted everyone else to see the Meryl I saw. For them to realize what a sham she was. And on top of that, maybe I could finally win a competition for once."

On the surface, it made a weird kind of sense. I could see the intention, at least — even if it had gone horribly wrong. "Why was winning this particular competition so important to you? You could have done it at any time, right?"

Coral's face clouded over once more. "As you can probably tell, I'm still quite young. I just got out of culinary school, in fact. Been trying to get a job, even tried to start up my own little catering gig on the side, but nothing's really taken off so far. You can imagine how my parents feel about that. Since I'm still swamped with student loans, I was living with them, hoping I could save up enough for a new place..."

"They put you up to this?" I finished.

"Not exactly," Coral said. "Well, yes and no. They always pushed me to apply to every competition I could, but this one was especially important. With the prize money, I could finally move out. I could finally start my own life for myself, not for them."

That, I could certainly empathize with. My mother and I were on two ends of the same spectrum, and moving out was one of the greatest decisions I ever made. Unfortunately, not everyone had that privilege. "So, what happened?"

"We had a bit of a fight before I left. Things had been coming to a head for a while now, but I wish they would have waited until after the competition..." She trailed off, her gaze distant and flecked with tears. "The details aren't important, but they basically kicked me out. Told me not to come back home." Coral shrugged. "I was really banking on the prize money to keep me going."

I sucked in a breath. Not having a place to go home to had always been one of my greatest fears as well, and if her story was anything to go on, she'd been through a lot more than that.

Taking a step closer, I knelt down next to her and put a tentative hand on her shoulder. She didn't flinch away. "Look," I started, still trying to find the words. "I don't know your parents, and I don't know your relationship with them, but if you ask me? Maybe it's good that you will be free of them."

Coral let out a sad, choking laugh. Well, to be honest, it was more of a laugh mixed with sobs. Tears ran freely down her face now. She sniffed and tried to wipe her eyes with her sleeve. "I just...I guess I was too desperate for their approval. Too desperate to be loved."

Putting aside the incident itself, there was a woman clearly in pain. She was still so young, with her whole life in front of her. Coral had plenty of talent — that much was for certain. Shame it had been used as a tool against her.

"I guess you understand why I can't get caught now. I don't have anything or anyone left. I thought this was my way out, but it backfired. Now what do I have?" She buried her face in her hands.

I thought for a moment, trying to figure out how to console her. What she did was wrong, there was no doubt about that. She would have to answer for her crimes, but that didn't mean she couldn't find a second chance. I wanted that for everyone — no matter what they'd done.

"I had a friend," I started, thinking of Will's predicament not too long ago, "who ended up in a similar situation as you. Doing bad things for good reasons."

"What happened to him?" She sniffed.

"He was arrested, yes. But with all the details of the situation out in the open, and because he told the truth to the police, he was able to get a lessened sentence. He'll be out less than a year from today, and the sheriff's already offered to help him find a job when he comes back."

She looked up at me with red, puffy eyes. "It could be worse...I guess."

"It could. But right now, the best thing you can do is own up to your mistakes. Fabio is gone, nothing will undo that, but you can still make sure his death isn't in vain. His family will want to know what happened. His wife." I paused, considering, before adding the last part. "Meryl will want to know too."

Coral groaned. It turned into a wail as she brought her knees up to her chest and buried her face. "It's not fair," she mumbled, barely audible. "After all this, Meryl gets off scot-free while I go down because of a misfired spell."

An idea struck me. One that, perhaps, could help both of us. "I have an idea." I tapped her on the shoulder. She looked up, dazed.

"What? Shouldn't you be calling the PEA so we can get this over with?"

"Let me make you a deal."

She raised her head a little further. "A deal? Like what?"

"If you cooperate with the PEA, I'll make sure they investigate Meryl's dealings as well."

Coral's eyes widened. "You'd do that?"

I nodded. "I want the same things you want, Coral. You can trust me." I extended my hand and looked her dead in the eye. "Can you do that?"

She hesitated. "Why would you help me? I ruined everything. My stupid curse..." Coral's face scrunched up again. "I killed someone!"

"Yes," I said simply. "You did. There's no denying that, but do I think you're a monster because of it? No. It's not like you came here *intending* to kill anyone. It was a stupid decision, yes, but the circumstances made it even worse than it needed to be. You seem like a good girl, Coral. Deep down. I want to help you...but you're going to have to take responsibility for what happened."

Coral wiped her eyes one more time, then outstretched her right hand to clasp mine. "Thank you, Kat." She whispered. "That means a lot to me."

Even after all that, my gambit was far from over. There was still the PEA to contend with — the *real* PEA.

If my theory was correct, they'd come along and realize that there was a rogue agent on the loose.

If it wasn't, well...

I didn't want to think about it.

I stood by Coral's side as she invoked the confession ritual. Any witch willingly "turning themselves in" for a crime would summon the PEA immediately.

Hopefully, the *real* PEA this time.

The agent appeared faster than I thought possible. He stepped out of the shadows in full suit-and-tie, not a hair out of place.

"Miss Sweetleaf," he announced. "Is it true that you have invoked the Confession Ritual? What is the nature of your crime?"

"You should know already," Coral said, staring at

her feet. "Your men were already here, scouring the place."

The agent frowned. "Excuse me, Miss Sweetleaf." He paused. "What men?"

I knew it! "I think you have a rogue agent on the loose, Mister...?"

"Carritage. Ralph Carritage, special agent." He extended his gloved hand. "And you are..."

"Kat Sullivan." I accepted the handshake, then looked down at my cat. "This is my familiar, Albus."

"I see." Guess it was true what they said about the PEA agents. They had one demeanor, and one only: business. "Now what was this about a rogue agent?"

"There was someone here, not long ago," Coral pointed out. "He claimed to be from the PEA. Said the town was under investigation. He questioned us and everything. You know anything about that?"

Agent Carritage rubbed his chin. His eyebrows drooped downward and creased his forehead. "Whoever was here certainly wasn't on my authority. I would have heard something about it. Do you remember the man's name?"

"Kaspar Hunt," I offered. "Though it could be an alias."

"Can't say I know anyone by that name, but thank you for the tip. I'll pass this up the line and investigate immediately. I trust you didn't provide this impostor with too much sensitive information?"

"Um..."

"I see." Agent Carritage said again. I was starting to think that was his favorite phrase. "This does complicate things." He flipped a page in his notebook, wrote something down, and drew a large circle around it. "Both of you, please come with me."

"Wait." I held up a hand. "How do we know you're not an impostor, too?"

"Besides the fact that I was able to respond to Miss Sweetleaf's Rite of Confession? I have my badge and ID number right here if you're unsure—" He flipped open his suit jacket and pulled out a small wallet, handing it over to me.

Special Agent Ralph Carritage, Paranormal Enforcement Agency ID #C271828

A stamped seal at the bottom was certified by Chief Warlock Cornelius Kane.

I passed it to Coral, who looked at it, nodded, and handed the wallet back to Agent Carritage.

"You must understand our skepticism," Coral said. "Especially given the recent intrusion."

"Of course," Agent Carritage agreed. "If we're all ready, then. Please come with me." He gestured at Albus. "The familiar, too."

"Where are we going?" Coral asked. She rubbed her arms as if cold.

"I don't know who or what that man you talked to was, but a colleague and I have an office just outside town. We'll meet there and you can tell me everything." His eyes flicked between us. "Don't worry, you'll be free to go afterward. Won't take more than an hour or two."

I took a deep breath. Coral placed her hand in mine. Albus followed along between us. Perhaps we both could get what we wanted here today.

CHAPTER TWENTY-FIVE

Gotta say, that second meeting — with the actual PEA agent this time — went so much more smoothly than the previous one. Agent Carritage and his partner, Agent Quin, made factory machines look slow and unpredictable. They rattled through dozens of questions, we filled out endless forms, and that was that.

Coral and I both had a chance to report Meryl's activities, and Coral explained the full nature of her involvement in Fabio's death. I was proud of her, in a way — she'd taken something that would ruin most people's lives and used it as a catalyst for change.

And, as morbid as it might sound, she wouldn't have to worry about finding a place to stay in the near future.

Agent Carritage offered me a ride home after all

was said and done. I wanted to refuse, but after the day I'd had? I was too tired to care.

We arrived back at my house in Haven around dinner time. When I got out of the car and thanked the agent, I noticed another familiar car parked across the street.

Was that...?

"Kat?" The voice startled me and I jumped, grabbing onto my fence for support. I turned to see Sheriff Cooper walking toward me, a pizza box and bottle of wine in hand.

Did I miss a memo or something? What was he doing here?

Oh.

"Kat, is that you?" He approached, a nervous smile on his face. "Thank goodness I caught you. Was starting to get worried."

I tilted my head. "You were worried about me?"

"Well, sure." He said it like it was obvious. "You're a hard woman to find these days."

"What are you talking about?" A cool gust brushed past us and I pulled my coat closer. "If we're going to talk anymore, let's go in, at least. It's cold out."

Cooper nodded. "Lead the way."

The short walk down the sidewalk and up the path to my front door didn't give me much time to think. This was so not a good time, but he had a point. I had been avoiding him. It wasn't just him, though. I'd been avoiding pretty much everyone lately.

Too bad I couldn't explain what had really been going on.

Albus gave a very persistent meow as we approached the door, and its meaning wasn't lost on me. It was one of those *what the heck are you doing* moments, and to be honest? I wasn't exactly sure.

Maybe it was the smell of the pizza and my growling stomach. Maybe it was the desire to talk to someone normal for a change. Someone who wasn't tied up in all this magical madness. Whatever the reason, I opened the door and led him inside.

"So you just *happened* to be in my part of the neighborhood with a pizza and a bottle of wine, is that right?" I teased him as I took off my coat and ushered Albus in.

Cooper laughed. He followed me into the kitchen and set the pizza and wine on the counter. I pulled out two glasses and turned back around to face him. "What do you want, Hal?"

He leaned against the counter, hands in his pockets. The hint of a smile crept across his face. "It's been a long time since we've been able to just sit around and talk, the both of us. I was actually going to take this pizza home with me tonight, but I was driving through the neighborhood on my way home and I figured, why not come check in on you?"

"Uh-huh." I wasn't buying it. Still, the thought that someone was actually concerned about me? It felt pretty nice. Instead of over-analyzing the situation, I focused on pouring two glasses of white wine. I think I deserved it after everything I'd been through lately.

"Come on, let's go sit down. The pizza's getting cold." I tilted my head into the living room. I carried the wine glasses, he carried the pizza box. We plopped down on the couch, flipped on the tv, and dug in.

No pretense. No expectation. Just like old times.

He didn't ask where I'd been or what I'd been up to, though I could see the questions all over his face. He respected my privacy enough not to press, though, and I respected that.

We spent the evening in quiet companionship. We shared the pizza, drank the wine, and laughed at a terrible monster movie on television. I could have read more into it, but what did it matter?

For one night, we were just here. Just relaxing. Enjoying each other's company. For one night, there was no evil magic lingering in the air, no scheming werewolves still on the loose, no nosy paranormal police.

It all felt so...normal.

And I think that's just what I needed right now. Just what both of us needed, if I was reading him right. I knew the event had been tough on their police department too, with the influx of visitors and traffic.

This was one night where no words needed to be shared.

At least, until Cooper fished an envelope out of his jacket and handed it over to me. "I don't know how to say this...but I thought you ought to know." He folded his hands in his lap and pursed his lips. "I don't mean to spoil the evening, but it's just come across my desk and I could use some help if you're up to it."

My heart suddenly in my throat, I opened the envelope and unfolded the letter inside.

It was a plea for help from Kelly Wilder.

Chance was missing.

From Morgan Vale:
Uh oh...things aren't looking so good for Chance

and the Wilders. Will Kat team up with Sheriff Cooper to find out what happened?

And will she be able to keep her magical secret from him long enough to save the day?

Find out in *Tricks and Trials*, book 4 in the most binge-worthy paranormal cozy mystery series.

Buy Tricks and Trials now.

Made in the USA
Coppell, TX
31 January 2024

28432638R00135